REWIND TO YESTERDAY

Also by Susan Beth Pfeffer

REWIND TO YESTERDAY

Susan Beth Pfeffer

Illustrated by Andrew Glass

Delacorte Press

To Linda, Ted, Josh, Mia, and David Israel

Published by
Delacorte Press
The Bantam Doubleday Dell Publishing Group, Inc.
666 Fifth Avenue
New York, New York 10103

Library of Congress Cataloging in Publication Data

Pfeffer, Susan Beth, 1948–
    Rewind to yesterday / by Susan Beth Pfeffer.
        p.   cm.
    Summary: After eleven-year-old Kelly discovers how
to set her family's new VCR so that it sends her back in
time, she and her twin brother Scott argue over how the
secret should be used.
    ISBN 0-440-50048-6
    [1. Video tape recorders and recording—Fiction.
  2. Twins—Fiction. 3. Science fiction.] I. Title.
PZ7.P44855Re 1988
[Fic]—dc19   88-6417
                                                       CIP
                                                        AC

Manufactured in the United States of America

September 1988

10 9 8 7 6 5 4 3 2 1

BG

⊚ CHAPTER 1

Kelly Diane Forrest pounded her fist on her math text-book. "I hate school!" she cried. "I hate everything about it, and I especially hate math."

Her best friend, Miri Weisberg, moved the book away from Kelly and laughed. "It's only September," she said. "How are you going to feel by March?"

"Worse," Kelly grumbled. "I can't even imagine how much worse I'll feel by then."

"Nobody feels good in March," Miri's grandfather, Pop, said. The two girls were in his newspaper shop, where they'd gone to check on his latest shipment of comics and candy bars. "March is for the birds. All slushy and gray. Give me September anytime."

"Sure, you'd say that," Kelly said to Pop. "You don't have to start school in September. At least by March you can pretend it's going to be summer soon. By March I'm counting the days until school ends."

"I thought you started that the day it begins," Miri said.

"I do," Kelly admitted. "But by March it has more meaning."

The girls giggled, and Pop grinned as well. Kelly and Miri had been best friends forever, or at least since they were both four and Kelly's parents had bought the house next door to Miri's family. It was as impossible for Kelly to imagine a world without Miri as it would be for her to conceive of one without Scott, her twin brother.

"Don't you think school is boring?" Kelly asked Miri for what was probably the thousandth time. "Don't you wish you were through with it already?"

"No," Miri answered for the thousandth time. "I like school. I like the idea of going for years and years more. Then when I can't go to school any longer, I'll teach it."

"What about you, Pop?" Kelly asked. "Did you hate school when you were a kid?"

"I liked it," Pop replied. "But I had to leave early to earn some money."

"My problem is I want to be an explorer," Kelly said. "And to be an explorer you have to have lots of degrees."

"The only thing left to explore is space," Pop said. "It used to be if you had a ship, you were in business. But it's all space shuttles and rockets now, and for them you have to know what you're doing."

"I want to travel through the stars," Kelly said. "And meet aliens and find suns and planets nobody even knows exist. I want to be the first person out of our galaxy."

"You want to find a planet where you won't have to go to school anymore," Miri said. "Admit it."

"My dream planet," Kelly said. "You stay home and teach, Miri. I'll send you postcards from outer space."

There was a loud charging sound at the door, which could only mean Scott was about to join them. "Kelly, come on home," he said as he ran into the shop. "You won't believe what Dad got."

"What'd he get?" Kelly asked, gathering her schoolbooks.

"A VCR," Scott said. "He finally bought one."

"Wow," Kelly said. "Miri, come on. Let's go see it."

"Bye, Pop," Miri said, giving him a quick kiss on the cheeks before joining Kelly and Scott as they sprinted home.

Sure enough, Kelly's father was attaching the VCR wires to the TV set as they joined him. Kelly's mother was sitting on the sofa, reading the instruction booklet to him as he worked.

"You really got one!" Kelly shouted when she saw the shiny new machine. "Oh, Daddy!"

"It was on sale," her father said. "They were practically giving them away."

Kelly's mother raised her eyebrows. "It cost enough," she said. "And it's an extravagance, but why not? We were bound to get one eventually, I suppose."

"How does it work, Dad?" Scott asked, moving behind the TV to join his father in the maze of wires.

"Frankly, I think it's magic," his father replied. "But I can tell you what it does. It tapes one thing when you're watching something else. And you can tape a show or a movie so you can watch it again. Or you can rent tapes, and see things that aren't on TV."

"And you can set it for the future," Kelly said. "Right, Dad? You can set it for a week from now, to tape some show you want to see but can't because you won't be home."

"I'm afraid not, honey," her father said. "We can preset the machine all right, but only for a single day."

"Not a week?" Kelly asked, trying not to sound disappointed.

"Just twenty-four hours," her father replied. "That's why it was so reasonably priced. We can preset the machine for one show every twenty-four hours."

"We really don't need any more than that," her mother said. "It isn't like we're jet-setters, always flying off to Paris. This way if some great old movie is on late at night, we'll be able to tape it and watch it the next day."

"Sure," Kelly said. She knew her mother was right, but still she'd dreamed about a machine you could program way into the future. She supposed that when she got around to traveling through space, she'd have a VCR that could be set to tape years in advance. She'd need one like that then. As long as she was stuck in school, though, twenty-four hours was enough.

"Is it set, Dad?" Scott asked.

"Let's find out," his father said. "Okay, turn on channel 2, just to be arbitrary about it, and we'll see if we can tape channel 13 at the same time."

"Put the button on the TV setting," Kelly's mother said, lifting her head up from the manual.

"Okay," Kelly's father said. He put a tape in the machine, pressed a couple of buttons, and soon the machine was making a cheerful whirring noise.

They waited impatiently for a minute, and then Kelly's father stopped taping, rewound what he'd done, and began playing the tape. Sure enough, the picture on the TV was nothing like what they'd been watching on channel 2. Just to be on the safe side, Kelly's father flipped over to channel 13, once the tape had ended, and sure enough, there was the show they'd just been watching on tape.

"It is magic," Miri said.

"Magic costs less," Kelly's mother said. "But it is fun. I can't wait until they show some great old Bogart movie at two in the morning and I'll know that I'm not missing it." She grinned with pleasure.

"I want to see the switches," Kelly declared, but as she raced over to the machine to get a better look, her arm brushed against the end-table lamp. She just barely caught it before it fell to the floor.

"Kelly, be careful," her father said. "Watch where you're going."

"I'm sorry," Kelly said. "I just wanted to see better."

"The VCR is not a toy," her father said. "I don't want you kids to play with it as though it were one."

"Actually, it is a toy," Kelly's mother said. "It just happens to be an expensive one. So be extra careful."

"I'm not sure they're old enough to play with it," Kelly's father said. "Not without one of us in the room to supervise."

"Hank, the kids all work computers," Kelly's mother said. "If they can run a computer, they can run a VCR."

"I'll be careful," Scott said. "And I'll make sure Kelly and Miri are too."

"I'm not worried about Miri," his father said, and smiled at her. "Miri could perform major surgery on me and I wouldn't worry. But you and your sister break everything in your path. I've seen hurricanes with less destructive power."

"I swear I won't break it ever," Kelly said. "If I do, you can put me in an orphanage."

"Don't tempt me," her father said. "All right. Just remember what I'm like when something I care about breaks."

Kelly remembered how her father had been when his new car had gotten its first dent. She shuddered at the thought.

"Good," her father said. "I can see you know what I'm talking about."

"Let's play with it some more," Scott said, and soon his father was showing all of them how the machine worked, and they were taping one thing and watching another, and presetting the machine to record for five minutes in the future, just for the practice. It was the most wonderful toy Kelly had ever seen, and she knew it was going to be just one more wonderful temptation when she was doing her homework.

Miri stayed over for supper, and then went back to her house. Kelly and Scott went to their rooms and finished their homework. Kelly was curled up in bed reading a mystery when Scott knocked on her door and came in.

"I just wanted to tell you to be careful with the VCR," Scott said. "I know how much it cost, and Dad'll kill you if you break it."

"Why should you care?" Kelly asked. She was two minutes older than Scott and didn't like it when he ordered her around.

"Because sometimes when you do something wrong, I get blamed too," Scott pointed out. "Like that time last summer when you stayed out too late. Dad changed both our curfews to eight, even though I was home where I was supposed to be all the time."

"I know what you mean," Kelly said. "Remember last winter when you broke the window, and we both had to pay to get it fixed?"

"That was your fault too," Scott said. "You were the one who dared me to throw the rock."

"I didn't think you could throw it that far," Kelly said. "You're stronger than I thought."

"And you're dumber," Scott said. "So be careful, okay? Otherwise, the only one of us who'll be able to use the machine will be Miri, when she isn't performing surgery."

Kelly giggled. "Did you see the way Dad kept looking at the VCR?" she asked. "Like he'd invented it."

"I know," Scott said. "Actually, it probably doesn't
matter what you want to do to it. Dad'll be playing
with it so much, we'll never have a chance."

"I'll be good if you are," Kelly said. It was a promise
she had made with Scott a lot of times. They both
took it seriously.

"I will be," he said. "Did you get all the math problems?"

"I got enough," Kelly said. "Don't make me think
about them again, okay?"

"You'd better get them all," Scott declared. "Or
else your grades'll go down, and Dad'll blame the
VCR, and then neither one of us will be allowed to
use it."

"You worry too much," Kelly said, and buried her
nose in her mystery to show Scott how little she cared.
She must have convinced him, since he left the room
without another word.

Kelly finished reading the chapter, put the book
down, and turned off her light. Scott was right, and
she knew it. Scott was right about a lot of things like
that. She did have to finish her math problems and
she'd better be careful about the VCR. Otherwise everything that should be fun would just be trouble.

She fell asleep almost immediately, but she kept
having dreams about her math homework being on
videotape. Finally, at five, she gave up trying to sleep.
She knew she'd be better off finishing her math and
then grabbing another hour's sleep before she had to

get up for school. So she got out of bed, put on her robe, and tiptoed downstairs to find her math book.

She sat down at the dining-room table and worked at the three unsolved problems. It was a real shame that explorers had to know math, she thought as she went over her answers. But they definitely did. A lot of exploring might be luck, but most of it involved knowing your math. There was no reason to believe that would be any different in outer space.

Kelly closed her math book and thought about going back to bed. She knew she ought to, but she wasn't tired anymore. Besides, the house was so much fun when everybody else was asleep. It felt like she owned it then, when it was quiet and dark.

And this was the best chance she'd ever have to play with the VCR. It would sure shut Scott up if Kelly knew how to run it perfectly while he was still reading the manual, trying to remember which button to push when. If she went back to bed, all she'd get was another hour's sleep. But if she stayed up, she'd get smarter. And smarter was always better than sleep.

So she went into the living room and turned on a light. The world outside was completely dark. It was almost as though she were the only person left alive in the world. She knew that wasn't true, that in just a half hour Pop would be waking up next door to get ready to open his shop by seven. And by the time Pop's store was open, Kelly's whole family and Miri and her mother would be up and around, getting ready for school and their jobs. But for now the world was dark, and Kelly owned it.

She read through the manual, impressed with how much of it she could remember from that evening's lesson with her father. The VCR was easy, much easier than the computer she used at school. She couldn't figure out what everybody was so worried about. There was no way she was going to break it, not unless she picked it up and threw it at somebody. Probably Scott, for making her worry so.

Kelly turned the TV on, keeping the sound low, and practiced taping one thing while watching another. Then she taped the show she was watching, and pressed the pause button at just the right moments so she could edit out the commercials. Then she rewound the tape, and watched all the different things the family had taped that evening. They must have taped a half dozen different snips of shows, practicing with the machine.

Kelly pressed the eject button, and the tape slid out. She put it in its box, and was about to put the box away and go back to bed, when she decided to practice presetting just one more time. So she set the machine for 6:00 and for five minutes. Only then she realized she'd set it for 6:00 P.M. when she'd meant to set it for 6:00 A.M. She got confused for the moment about how to change the time around, and without really thinking about it, she pressed the rewind button, even though there was no tape in the machine to rewind.

But by the time she realized that, Kelly felt her stomach getting whooshy, and she felt light-headed, almost as though she were floating. She kept pressing

the rewind button, feeling somehow that if she could hold on to that, she'd stay on earth.

And then for a second things got dark, as if her eyes were closed and she couldn't get them open. But then things got light again, and Kelly found herself standing across the room from the VCR. Her parents and Scott and Miri were there, and her mother was talking about watching old Bogart movies that were on at two in the morning.

"I want to see the switches," Kelly declared, but something inside her clicked, and she knew what had happened next, how she'd almost knocked over the lamp. So she was careful as she walked over to the machine and didn't even come near to knocking anything over. Instead of her father scolding her and telling her the VCR wasn't a toy, he showed her which was the rewind button and which was fast forward.

It was without a doubt the strangest experience Kelly had ever lived through, and that included the time Scott had put the toad in her bathwater. She knew just what had happened, and what was happening, but she still felt odd and mystified, and hadn't the slightest idea what she had made happen, when her stomach got unsettled again, and her head felt like it was made of helium, and everything went dark, and then she was back in her living room, at six in the morning, with the world still dark and alone and quiet.

Kelly ran from the machine and straight back to her bedroom. Something extremely weird had just happened, and she wasn't about to figure out what it was in a cold dark house with nobody to help her.

⊚ CHAPTER 2

Kelly spent the morning in school trying to think about her work, and not succeeding. Fortunately, her teachers didn't notice her distracted look, so they didn't call on her. She tried to concentrate on science and social studies, but her mind kept going back to that strange whooshy feeling and her growing conviction that she had somehow managed to travel through time.

She knew she was going to have to try it again, to prove to herself that she really had done it, before she even thought about letting anyone else in on her secret. Not that she was about to tell just anybody. Her parents, for starters, must never know. It would be just like them to return the machine because it was defective. And she didn't trust Scott either. So the only person she knew she could tell was Miri, but even Miri couldn't be told until Kelly had proven to herself that the whole experience wasn't just a dream.

With all that on her mind, it was no wonder geography didn't hold her attention. Usually Kelly enjoyed geography, since she liked to imagine herself going to all those exotic places. But her mind was on a different form of travel, and there was no place on earth that could equal it for excitement.

She had lunch at 11:32, the same time she always did, only this time she made a point of checking her digital watch carefully to confirm the time. She and Miri both got the macaroni and cheese, and Kelly deliberately bought two containers of milk, as well as a slice of pie. She never bought more than one milk at lunch, which was why she made such a big point to herself of buying two. Just buying the two milks made her feel scientific.

"What are you doing after school today?" she asked Miri, who was gobbling down the macaroni and cheese. It was one of the few lunches they served at school that was close to edible.

"I'm going to the store to help Pop," Miri said. "Want to come?"

"Not today," Kelly said, happy for the first time in her life that Miri had other plans. It was all working out perfectly. Tuesday was Scott's soccer practice day, and her parents wouldn't get home from work until after five. She had at least an hour then to be alone, just her and the VCR. She stared at her two milk containers to prove that she really had bought two.

"What'll you do?" Miri asked.

"Oh, I don't know," Kelly said. "Maybe I'll get my homework done early. It drives Scott crazy if I have mine done before Mom and Dad get home and he doesn't."

"You're such a good sister," Miri said, but Kelly just grinned. She might not be a great sister, but she certainly was a smart one, and what she was up to was none of Scott's business. Not until she decided he was ready to learn the truth, and that probably would be when she won the Nobel Prize for physics. She assumed physics was the right category. If it wasn't, they could just make one up for her. Because the one thing Kelly was sure of was that she was the first person ever to travel through time by way of a VCR.

"Do you remember yesterday, when Dad brought the VCR home?" Kelly asked, trying to sound casual about it.

"Of course I do," Miri said. "Why? Did you break it or something?"

"No, of course not," Kelly said, but she blushed anyway. "I was just wondering if you remembered whether my father gave us some kind of lecture about being careful with the machine."

"Of course he did," Miri said. "No worse than usual though."

Kelly licked her lips. "Was there a reason, do you think? I mean, did I do something dumb like almost knock over a lamp? I was so excited about the VCR, I've kind of forgotten what happened."

Miri gave Kelly a long look. "You didn't knock anything over," she replied. "But you sound like something hit you on the head. What do you mean you don't remember what happened last night? You always remember everything."

Kelly shrugged her shoulders. "School was so exiting this morning, it pushed everything else from my mind," she said, trying not to show her excitement. Miri didn't remember her almost knocking over the lamp. That must mean that when Kelly went back in time, she'd corrected what had happened. She had changed the past. It wasn't complete proof, but it was as close as she could figure out how to get without giving away her secret.

"Are you going to drink that extra milk?" Miri asked.

Kelly looked up with a start. "Why?" she asked, not at all sure what she should answer.

"Because if you aren't, I will," Miri replied. "Otherwise I'll go back in line and get another one for myself. That's all."

"I'm drinking it then," Kelly said. She opened the carton, stuck her straw in it, and took a sip. She had no desire to drink the extra milk, and as if to prove it, she swallowed the wrong way and began to cough.

"You okay?" Miri asked.

Kelly managed to nod. "Get your milk," she choked out. "I'm fine."

So Miri got up, and Kelly managed to stop coughing. If nothing else, she at least had a strong reason to remember that she'd bought two milks. And that was the important thing. Explorers had to risk death all the time, although Kelly suspected she would have been the first to die from swallowing milk in a school cafeteria.

The rest of the school day inched along. It drove Kelly crazy that she had to be in classes when she should be home conducting her noble experiment. Coming close to death at lunch had proven to her the importance of what she was up to and the need to make notes, so that if she did get lost in a time warp, the world would know what had happened to her. Not to mention her parents, who got upset when she was late for anything. At least if they knew she was late because of science, they might not ground her, if she ever made it back into their time dimension. Kelly decided she'd worry later about what would happen if she didn't make it back into their time dimension after school.

Eventually the final bell rang, and Kelly seized her freedom and ran straight home. She made it back there in record time, and sure enough there was no sign of life either at her house or next door.

"I had lunch at 11:32," she told herself. "I bought two milks, and I choked on the second one." She looked around the house for a notebook to put her experiment down on and finally realized she had one in her hands. So she tore out a piece of loose-leaf paper, and with trembling fingers she wrote what had happened to her that morning. She wasn't sure she'd be able to construct just how she'd managed to travel through time, but it came back to her as she wrote. There was no tape in the VCR, and she'd preset the machine for a certain time and length, and then she'd held on to the rewind button. Kelly was surprised how clear the memory was, now that she was putting it down on paper. She felt scientific as she wrote, very Nobel Prizish. The world of science would owe her one big debt, and Kelly had every intention of being gracious about it. She'd be the youngest person by far to win the Nobel Prize, she figured, and probably after she did, she wouldn't have to go to school again. Who could possibly be qualified to teach her, even in high school? She'd go on all the talk shows instead, and maybe star in the movie version of her life. What she was about to do was the biggest thing ever to happen on earth, she thought as she put the sheet of paper down on top of the TV set. Her parents would be sure to find it there, if she did screw up and ended up in some giant inescapable Elsewhere. If she never came back, she hoped her parents would tell the world about the sacrifice she'd made, and maybe they could name a scholarship fund for her.

For the first time that day, Kelly got scared. It was one thing to travel through time by accident. It was something else altogether to do it on purpose. Besides, she still didn't have absolute proof that she had traveled. Miri might simply have forgotten that she'd almost knocked over the lamp. It couldn't have been nearly as important to her as it was to Kelly. Or maybe Kelly dreamed the part about the lamp and the rest was what had really happened. There were a lot of variables with time travel.

She knew she was going to need some more proof, something other than her conviction that she'd bought two containers of milk and had choked on the second one. And then Kelly figured out what she could do. The milks each cost a quarter. If she went back in time, and bought only one milk, she should come back to the real world one quarter richer.

Kelly walked over to the closet and got out her jacket. She had thirty-five cents, one quarter and two nickels. With trembling fingers, she put the three coins down on the TV set by the page with her notes on her experiment. She thought about writing the amount down, but that seemed too confusing. If she changed time after all, wouldn't the sheet of paper change, too, and just say she'd left behind sixty cents instead? She was simply going to have to know in her heart of hearts that she had only thirty-five cents, and if she came back and found sixty, then that was going to be proof enough for her.

It was 11:32, she told herself. For a moment she couldn't remember whether it was A.M. or P.M. but then she laughed at herself. Of course it was A.M. Kelly rubbed her hands together, had an image flash through her mind of sterilizing them, as if she were readying for surgery, and then managed to laugh. She was only doing what she had done that morning. If she'd succeeded then without knowing what she was doing, it was bound to be a piece of cake to do it now.

Still, there was risk, and she was a fool if she didn't know it. So Kelly went back to her sheet of paper and wrote, I love you Mom and Dad at the bottom of the sheet. You, too, Scott, she added after a moment's hesitation. "And Miri." If she never came back, at least they'd have that to remember her by.

Kelly asked herself one last time if she really wanted to try something that could end up with her never coming back. But she knew she had to. Explorers always took risks. They left assuming they would return, but there were no guarantees. So she swallowed hard, looked around the living room, just in case it was the last time she'd ever see it, and then walked over to the VCR.

Lunch started at 11:32, she told herself, and she choked on the milk at 11:54. So she set the machine for 11:30, and put it down for half an hour's worth of recording time. She made sure there was no tape in the machine, and then she closed her eyes, prayed she'd return home safely, set the machine to preset, and held on to the rewind button.

It hit Kelly first again in her stomach, which felt as though she were riding the world's biggest fastest roller coaster. And then the light-headedness hit, and she held on to the rewind button with whatever strength she had left. It was as if she were flying; her legs no longer seemed to be touching ground. Then things got dark again, even though this time it was broad daylight and there was no reason for everything to be so black.

And then, as suddenly as things had gotten dark, they were light again, and Kelly found herself sitting in her classroom. That's not right, she thought to herself. I should be in the cafeteria. But even as she thought that, the bell rang, and she joined the rush of kids to make it down the hall to the cafeteria line.

Kelly told herself again and again to buy only one milk, and when she passed the cartons it seemed no big deal at all to take only one. She always bought only one anyway. She and Miri sat down, began eating their lunch, and talked about the exact same things they had talked about earlier. Kelly even brought up the question of whether she'd nearly knocked over the lamp the day before, and Miri gave her the same funny look.

Only this time Miri didn't ask if she could drink the second milk because there was no second milk. She just went back in line and got one for herself. She even asked Kelly if she wanted another one, too, which confused Kelly for the moment.

Was she supposed to say yes, she wondered, and then she realized that if she did, there would just be thirty-five cents on the TV set when she returned. So she turned Miri down, and sat there waiting for her to come back, and she didn't drink a second milk, and she didn't swallow the wrong way and suffer a coughing fit. Instead she looked around the cafeteria. Scott was sitting with his friends at a corner table, and Mark Horowitz was throwing spitballs at Donna Rodriguez. Kelly hadn't noticed any of those things the first time. She began to realize all the important ways time travel could be used. When she got back to real time, she decided, she would make a list.

Miri came back with her milk, and soon the girls were talking about the same things they'd talked

about originally. Kelly figured out then that time
travel could also be pretty boring. It wasn't that she
didn't enjoy talking with Miri, but she'd already heard
what Miri had to say. There was bound to be a lot of
repetition if you just kept going back to the same time
over and over again. Kelly wasn't sure how to handle
that problem.

But then she felt all whooshy again. She wondered
if Miri could tell, but she didn't seem to notice anything, and Kelly realized she was still talking as though
nothing had changed. Except that inside her body was
flying, and even though she could see that her mouth
was moving, and noises were coming out saying things
like "I'll see you later, Miri," the darkness was there,
and then it was light and Kelly was standing by the
TV set, holding on to the rewind button, and the
room was spinning, and she thought she was going to
throw up.

Only instead she let go of the button and sank to
the floor for a moment until everything stopped spinning around her. She looked at her watch. It had been
3:12 when she had begun the experiment, and now,
sure enough, it was 3:42.

Kelly was almost scared to get up. She knew what
she had to check next, the one that would prove to her
she really had traveled through time. She had left one
quarter and two nickels behind. There just had to be
another quarter there. That's all she needed, twenty-
five cents' worth of proof.

Kelly clenched her fists until she could feel her fin-
gernails cutting into her hands. Then she rose slowly,

dizzy for only a moment. The floor felt solid under her feet, and the living room was exactly as it always was. She could hear voices from the sidewalk in front of the house. Scott would be home soon. She'd better get the note off the TV set before he arrived. There was no point in his learning of her experiment just yet. There was certainly no point in his learning that she loved him.

She took two shaky steps toward the TV and closed her eyes, afraid to see what might be there. But then she forced herself to open them. There was the note she'd left, and she grabbed it fast and folded it. She'd need her notes for science, but the time wasn't right yet to tell the world. If there was only thirty-five cents on the TV, the time would never be right.

Kelly turned around so she would face the TV set. She made her eyes focus on the pile of coins. And there they were, two nickels and two quarters. Sixty cents where once there had been thirty-five.

Kelly grabbed the money and felt it over and over again in her hands. Four coins instead of three. No extra milk that day. No choking or coughing. Sixty cents. She had done it. She had traveled through time and changed the way things had happened. She had the quarter to prove it. The only thing left now was to demonstrate her secret to the world. She could only hope it would be used for the power of good.

⊚ CHAPTER 3

Kelly ran upstairs with her notes and her change and hid them under her mattress. There was no reason to believe anybody would be snooping around trying to find them, but she wasn't about to take any chances.

Then she realized she would need her money the next day for lunch, so she lifted the mattress up and pulled out the money. She wished she didn't have to, but there was no way of proving that the coins were the actual time-traveled money anyway, so there was no point in keeping them. Her notes got wrinkled from all the lifting and pulling, but that didn't matter. What she'd done was so amazing that wrinkled notes wouldn't be a problem.

Kelly went back down to the living room and put a tape in the machine, just in case anybody else felt like exploring with the VCR. She couldn't be positive that the machine had to be empty to time-travel, but if it did, she figured she'd stop anyone else who felt like trying.

She looked around the living room and marveled at how normal it all seemed. Twenty-four hours ago she hadn't even known about the VCR, and now she'd zipped around in time twice. She couldn't wait until she was on *The Tonight Show*.

· The next step, she decided, was to get a witness, and the one she wanted was Miri. Kelly still didn't trust Scott to know what she'd been up to. But if she ran to Pop's store and hijacked Miri, there might still be time for a demonstration before Scott got back from soccer practice.

So she grabbed her jacket, made sure she had her keys, and ran the few blocks to Pop's store. Kelly loved the store. Mostly it sold papers and candy, plus stuff like tissues and jigsaw puzzles. Once, though, Pop had gotten a consignment of bowling balls, and he'd sold them too. Pop didn't seem to care that the store wasn't about to make him or anybody else rich, but he wouldn't give it up. Miri's mother was always after him to retire, but Pop refused.

"I'm not ready to be an old man," he declared. "I don't want to sit around all day long watching game shows and complaining about gout."

So Pop kept his store open, but he had cut down on his hours a little. And Miri's mother continued to worry, and Miri continued to hang out there, helping whenever she could, and Kelly didn't blame her. The store was nicer than any place at the mall. It had character, and sometimes it had bowling balls.

"Hi, Kel," Miri said, looking up from behind the counter as Kelly entered the shop. "You here to spend money or just hang out?"

"I'm here to take you home," Kelly replied. "Where's Pop?"

"He's in the back doing inventory," Miri declared. "I can't leave for another half hour at least."

"Sure you can," Pop called from the back room. "The inventory's waited this long, it can wait another day."

"Pop, you said you had to get it done right away," Miri shouted back. "You said it was this week or never."

"So it'll be never," Pop said, and he joined Kelly and Miri in the front of the shop. "Believe me, with the kind of inventory I have, it's no big deal when it gets done."

"I like your attitude," Kelly said. "I feel the same way about my math homework."

"School's important," Pop said. "School counts for something. Pay attention to your classes, and then you can grow up and do something important with your life. Be a doctor. Help humanity."

"You don't have to go to school for all that," Kelly said. "Helping humanity, I mean. Some of the greatest humanity helpers could hardly even read."

"But the ones who could knew what the papers were writing about them," Pop said. "So keep on with school until you're at least smart enough to know how to find the best libel lawyers."

"I never thought about libel," Kelly said. "But I don't know what they could say about me anyway."

"They could say you didn't pass sixth-grade math unless you start really paying attention to it," Miri said. "I saw the way you were looking out the window all period today."

"I had things on my mind," Kelly said. "Important things. Miri, you just have to come home with me right now. It's really important."

"I want to stay and help Pop," Miri said. "I'll be home in an hour."

"An hour is way too late," Kelly said. "Pop, please fire Miri so she can come home with me."

"Miri, you're fired," Pop said. "At least until tomorrow. Go home this minute, and when your mother gets in, tell her I'll be home for supper."

"I'm going, I'm going," Miri grumbled. "But call me if you need me back here."

"She'll be at my house," Kelly said. "But don't call. We're going to be really busy."

"Call," Miri said, and gave her grandfather a kiss. "See you later, Pop."

"Don't get into mischief," Pop said, and waved good-bye to the girls.

"Kelly, what's going on?" Miri demanded as soon as they were on the street. "What's so important that you had to drag me out of there? Pop's never going to get his inventory done unless I'm there to help him. Did you have to run in like your house was on fire and make me go home early?"

"Miri, this is so important it just might be the most

important thing that happened in the whole world ever," Kelly declared. "And I'm not exaggerating either. The entire future of humanity is involved."

"Great," Miri said. "But don't think Mom is going to accept that as an excuse for my leaving early."

"Miri, listen to me," Kelly said. "First of all, walk faster. We've got to get home right away."

"I'm walking as fast as I can," Miri replied, but she did pick up her pace. "Okay, what's the most important thing that ever happened in the universe? I can hardly wait to find out."

"How many containers of milk did I have at lunch today?" Kelly asked.

Miri stood absolutely still. "Milk!" she shrieked. "Milk! You're asking me about milk?"

"This is important milk," Kelly said. "How many containers did I have? Think, Miri. This is so important that the entire future of the world is waiting on your answer."

"Some people's best friends aren't crazy," Miri said. "Some people have perfectly normal best friends. Friends who don't think how many containers of milk did they have for lunch is a life-and-death question."

"How many?" Kelly persisted.

"I don't know," Miri said. "One. That's what you always get, one. Why? How many do you think you got?"

"Two," Kelly said. "Do you remember me choking on one of them?"

"I'd like to choke you now," Miri replied. "No, I don't remember your choking on one. Satisfied?"

"Remember asking me for my second container?" Kelly asked. "Because I wasn't drinking it?"

"I thought you choked on it," Miri said. "Kelly, what's up? Does one of us have amnesia? If that's it, it's you and not me."

"Why do you say that?" Kelly said, hardly able to keep her excitement under control

"Because what I do remember from lunch today is your asking some weird questions about last night," Miri said. "About when your father brought home the VCR. Now you're asking about milk. Maybe you should see a neurosurgeon."

"I should probably see the President," Kelly said. "Do you think if I called him up, they'd let me make an appointment to see him?"

"I don't see why not," Miri replied. "I'm sure he has plenty of free time to see crazy eleven-year-olds."

"I don't know," Kelly said. "This thing is so big, I'm not sure how I want to handle it. I only know I want it to be used for peace. I mean like the President could push the button, you know, and then he could change his mind and we could save the entire world from destroying itself. Wow. I'd personally be responsible for the world not being blown up. I guess then I'd get the Nobel Peace Prize too."

"Too?" Miri said. "Kelly, what in heaven's name is going on with you?"

"You have to absolutely swear to secrecy," Kelly whispered. She glanced around for suspicious-looking people, but saw only the usual types going about their business.

"I absolutely swear," Miri said with a sigh. "Kelly, why is it every time you make me absolutely swear, I'm the one who ends up in trouble?"

"That's not true," Kelly said. "And in this case it certainly isn't. As a matter of fact, I'll see to it that you get some of those Nobel Prizes too. And they pay money. You can be as rich and famous as me, almost."

"Great," Miri said. "I wouldn't want to be too rich and famous. At least not until I'm twelve."

"That's just when you will be," Kelly said. "All right, Miri. If you're ready to be serious, I'll tell you what's going on."

"If I'm ready to be serious," Miri said. "I'm minding my own business, or at least I'm minding Pop's, and you think you should tell me to get serious. Is it serious to talk about how much milk you drank at lunch?"

"All this is about the milk," Kelly said. "That was my experiment, my way of proving it."

"Proving what?" Miri said. "Not that I want to know."

Kelly checked the streets out again. The only person within a block of them was Mrs. Gilhooley, and she was hard of hearing. "Time travel," Kelly whispered.

Miri stood still and turned around to face Kelly. "Time travel?" she repeated.

"Not so loud," Kelly said. "The world isn't ready yet."

"Neither am I," Miri said. "Kelly, it's all well and good to say you're going to explore outer space when you grow up, but that's no reason to act like a space cadet now."

"I'm telling you the truth," Kelly declared. "The most absolutely serious true truth you can imagine. I traveled through time. Twice. Once I went back to yesterday and didn't knock over the lamp. And today I went back to lunch and didn't get a second container of milk."

"Great," Miri said. "I'm glad you didn't waste your time on saving Abraham Lincoln's life or anything unimportant like that."

"I can't save Abraham Lincoln's life," Kelly declared. "At least I don't see how I can. The machine has only twenty-four-hour preprogrammable."

"Your time-travel machine," Miri said. "The one you've been building in your spare time with aluminum foil and paper clips."

"The VCR," Kelly said. "It has twenty-four-hour preprogrammable. How do you think I've been traveling through time?"

"Oh, I don't know," Miri said. "I thought maybe you'd been following white rabbits around through holes in the ground. Kelly in Weirdoland."

"I know this sounds strange to you," Kelly said. Miri laughed.

"Listen to me," Kelly said, and she grabbed Miri's jacket. "I'm serious, Miri. I did it. I traveled through time." She forced Miri to look at her, and she told her exactly what had happened, from waking up to do her math straight through finding the extra quarter on the TV set. "The thing is," she concluded, hoping Miri believed her, "is that it's the most wonderful thing that ever happened to me, but it's the scariest too. I don't think all VCRs are built so you can travel through time."

"No," Miri said. "I don't think they all are either."

"I'm telling you so you can travel through time too," Kelly said. "That way we'll both have done it, so when we call up the President there'll be two of us, and he'll have to believe us."

"I'd hold off on telling him," Miri said. "At least until after you've had a complete physical."

"You think traveling through time has altered my atoms?" Kelly asked. "I hadn't thought of that. You know how it is, you accidentally travel though time, and then that's all you want to do again. You don't think about your atoms."

"I was thinking about the atoms in your brain," Miri said. "The ones that used to be normal, and now are totally crazy. Kelly, I don't know what's going on, but I think you're very sick."

"That's why I have to prove to you that what I'm saying is true," Kelly replied. "So we're going to my house now, and I'll show you how to do it, and you can travel through time and change something too."

"I'd like to change this whole conversation," Miri said.

"Fine," Kelly said. "We can do that. You can talk to me about anything else you want. You can change things when you travel through time. It's amazing, Miri. I bet we end up on the cover of *People* magazine."

"So we're going to travel through time right now," Miri said. "We set the VCR and I hold on to the rewind button, and the next thing I know we're talking about potatoes instead of time travel. Right?"

"Exactly," Kelly said. "It makes you nauseous and dizzy, and things go dark, but it's worth it, so don't get scared."

"I won't, I promise," Miri said. "Oh, I guess Scott's going to time-travel with us."

"Oh no," Kelly said, spotting Scott on his bike a block ahead of them. "Not Scott! I don't want him to know. Not yet at least. I'll tell him before I tell the President, but not yet. Sorry, Miri."

"Then we won't go time-traveling today?" Miri asked. "I'll just go home and do my homework instead?"

"We'll do it tonight after everybody goes to sleep," Kelly said. "Come over to my house at midnight, and I'll show you then."

"You expect me to come over at midnight?" Miri asked. "I'm supposed to sneak out of my house and into yours, just so you can prove to both of us that you're totally crazy?"

"Yes," Kelly said. "Miri, if our friendship counts for anything, I'll see you tonight at midnight."

"Only if you promise me that when nothing happens, and we both make idiots of ourselves standing around holding on to your father's VCR, that you'll drop this whole stupid business and try to be a normal human being again," Miri said. "If you still remember how to be a normal human being."

"I promise," Kelly said. "Now go on home and act natural."

"It'll be an act," Miri said. "Good-bye, Kelly. See you at midnight."

"You won't be sorry," Kelly promised her. "Miri, you're about to be the second person ever to travel through time."

"Great," Miri said. "I'll be sure to bring an extra container of milk."

⊚ CHAPTER 4

Kelly got out of bed five minutes before midnight, just in case Miri was early. Both houses were dark, as she had assumed they would be.

She put on her robe and slippers and tiptoed downstairs. She could hear the stairs squeaking as she made her way down, and midway down she took her slippers off. That was a slight improvement. She was sure every breath she took would wake up her whole family, probably bring the police, too, and maybe the FBI. It occurred to her that for all she knew time travel was against the law.

Of course *she* wasn't about to travel through time, just Miri, so she supposed she was safe. The idea of Miri going to jail was so silly that Kelly began to giggle. It wasn't easy tiptoeing downstairs, holding on to her slippers and trying to keep from laughing out loud. The harder she tried not to laugh, the more she wanted to. Her body began to shake, which got the bannister rattling. Kelly felt like she was making enough noise to wake up half the people in town, but that only got her laughing harder. Eventually she bit down hard on her lower lip, and the pain was enough to calm her down. But she was never so relieved as when she made it into the living room, away from squeaking staircases and bedrooms with open doors.

According to the VCR's digital clock, it was 11:59. Kelly willed Miri to come right over, but it didn't work. By 12:02, Kelly was just about ready to go next door and drag Miri out of bed. She couldn't believe Miri was doing this to her, not to mention to science and the history of the universe.

But just as Kelly was deciding to open the door and go out, Miri appeared.

"What took you so long?" Kelly demanded in an angry whisper as she let Miri in.

"You mean why did I bother to come at all?" Miri replied. "I was sure the whole thing was a big dumb joke. And you didn't turn any lights on here, so I guessed I was just supposed to come over and you'd be sleeping away."

"I'd never do anything like that," Kelly said.

"I know," Miri replied with a sigh. "That's the only reason I'm here. You may be crazy, but you're not mean. So here I am. And there's the VCR. Is this supposed to be now, or are we traveling through time already?"

"Don't be silly," Kelly said. "Of course this is now. You'll know when it isn't. It feels different."

"Great," Miri said. "How different, besides making you sick to your stomach?"

Kelly shrugged her shoulders. "It's kind of hard to describe," she declared. "You know what's going to happen, but it's real exciting anyway, because you know if you just say one thing different then you've changed history. You'll know when you do it."

"I don't think history really changed because you only bought one milk," Miri said. "Are you sure we can't save Abraham Lincoln's life?"

"All we can change is the last twenty-four hours," Kelly replied. "Sorry if that isn't good enough for you."

"I suppose it'll have to be," Miri said. "Now are you sure you know what you're doing?"

"Trust me," Kelly said. "Once you've done it, Miri, you'll want to do it again and again."

"I trust you," Miri said, although it was obvious she didn't. Kelly decided to ignore Miri's skeptical look and pulled her over to the VCR.

"Now what time in the past twenty-four hours do you want to go back to?" Kelly asked.

"How about midnight last night?" Miri said. "I was nice and asleep then."

"You can't go back to when you were asleep," Kelly replied. "If you do that, you'll just sleep through your time travel and you won't even know you did it."

"This is very confusing," Miri said with a yawn. "You pick a time for me."

"How about when we were talking after school this afternoon," Kelly suggested.

"That was bad enough to live through once," Miri said. "I don't think I could take that conversation twice."

"How about your supper tonight?" Kelly asked. "Anything interesting happen then?"

"Not really," Miri said. "I told Mom and Pop about what happened in school today. Of course I didn't tell them how first you had two milks and then only one. We talked about my English assignment instead."

"Great," Kelly said. "Go back in time then and talk about something else."

"Why should I?" Miri asked. "Kelly, that's not exactly as important as saving Abraham Lincoln's life."

"How many times do I have to tell you we're not going to save Abraham Lincoln's life!" Kelly cried. "The only reason you're going back in time is to prove to yourself that you can. That's important enough for us right now."

"What's important to me is getting some sleep tonight," Miri declared. "I'm going back to bed, unless I still am in bed and this turns out to be just a dumb dream."

"Go back in time to supper," Kelly said. "And instead of talking about your English assignment, talk about your math instead. That's all. Did you talk about math, too, at dinner?"

"I don't know," Miri said. "I didn't take notes."

"You should have," Kelly said. "I do. All scientists make notes."

"I am not a scientist," Miri said. "And right now

I'd trade all those Nobel Prizes you offered me for a good night's sleep."

"You'll have plenty of time to sleep later," Kelly promised her. "Did anything happen in school today? Anything you really remember?"

Miri shook her head. "I had a very boring day," she said. "Just the way I like them."

"I know," Kelly said. "You must have watched something on TV tonight."

"I did," Miri said. "The *Margie Maclain Show*. It was pretty boring too."

"Fine," Kelly said. "We'll send you back in time to the *Margie Maclain Show*, only when you get back there, go to the kitchen and get something to eat. Did you do that during the show?"

"Not that I can remember," Miri said.

"Perfect," Kelly said. "Get an apple. Don't wait for the commercial or anything. Just get up and get an apple and eat it. Maybe even change the station as you walk to the kitchen. Do something different from what you did. Just one little change to see how it feels."

"Okay," Miri said. "I'll eat an apple. Now how am I supposed to get back there?"

"*Margie Maclain* is on from 8:00 to 8:30," Kelly said. "We'll set the machine for 8:05. There won't be a commercial on then. And we'll set it for ten minutes, to give you time to eat the apple. I don't think you should travel through time with food in your mouth. You'd probably just throw it up when you got back here. You'll feel kind of whooshy when the time is up, so don't keep on eating once you feel that way."

"This is very complicated," Miri said. "But if it'll shut you up, I guess it's worth it."

"It doesn't have to be an apple," Kelly told her. "You can eat something smaller if you'd like. Eat a few grapes and then go back into the living room and switch channels. That way you'll see something you never saw before, and you'll know you've traveled through time."

"Where will you be during all this?" Miri asked.

"I'm not sure," Kelly admitted. "I think I'll be right here waiting for you to get back, but maybe I'll be in my room doing my homework. That's where I was between 8:00 and 8:30. If I'm here, I'll be making notes."

"I'm scared," Miri said. "Either this is true, in which case I'm about to travel through time, or else my best friend is totally crazy. Or maybe I am, and this is all a hallucination. Or aliens from another planet have taken over our minds, and made us think this is really happening, when actually we're just their pawns."

"Stop imagining things," Kelly said. "Just go back in time and eat a few grapes. Once you've done it, you'll like it."

Miri sighed. "If I never come back, tell Mom and Pop I love them," she said. "And my book report is on my chest of drawers."

"You've already done your book report?" Kelly asked. "It isn't due until Friday."

"I believe in being prepared," Miri said. "Okay, Kelly. Let's get this over with."

So Kelly set the machine for 8:05 P.M. to run for ten minutes. She made sure there was no tape in the machine, put the timer on, and told Miri to hold the rewind button and not to let go.

At first Miri was there, holding on to the button, but looking kind of sick. And then she began to fade, and it almost looked as though her feet were no longer on the floor, and Kelly blinked, and Miri was no longer there.

"Wow," Kelly said. She could only hope everything worked out all right, and Miri came back in ten minutes. Otherwise she was going to have a lot of explaining to do. She'd never seen anybody actually disappear before, except on television, where it was obviously fake. And Miri was definitely gone. All at once, Kelly got scared.

She knew the next ten minutes were going to be endless, and she decided to do something about killing the time. First she went to the kitchen and opened up a bag of chocolate-chip cookies. She wolfed down a half dozen of them, getting crumbs all over everything. Kelly thought about sweeping them up, but that seemed like a frivolous chore when her best friend was traveling through time changing history. Kelly knew she was going to be asked what she'd been doing during Miri's time trip and she didn't want to have to answer that she was sweeping. So she left the crumbs and went back into the living room. Only two minutes had gone by. There were eight left to go before Miri either returned from the past or was never seen again. Eight long, terrifying minutes. Kelly went back to the kitchen and ate another six cookies.

She walked back to the living room then and got out her notebook. Obviously what she should be doing was making notes about Miri's trip. So she sat cross-legged on the sofa and tried to remember everything Miri had said about the *Margie Maclain Show* and how they had decided she should eat grapes and not apples and change the channel. Kelly wrote it down exactly as she remembered, although she was a little sorry Miri didn't come off better. The way it seemed to her, Kelly had practically had to shove Miri into time travel while Miri kept whining about not getting enough sleep. Kelly just hoped history wouldn't judge Miri harshly. After all, it had to be scary to be the second person to travel through time, especially if you weren't as naturally brave as the first person who had traveled.

Every thirty seconds Kelly checked the clock. The truth of the matter was, she had no idea what to do if Miri didn't return. She even got out the owner's manual for the VCR, just in case there was something in there about time travel that she had missed. But of course there wasn't. Kelly knew she was the one who had discovered how to do it, and the people who designed the machine probably weren't even aware of what they had created. The first person to mix blue and yellow together probably didn't know he'd invented green.

With two minutes left to go, Kelly put her notebook down and went back into the kitchen for the
cookies. She brought the bag with her and settled
down on the sofa to watch for Miri's return. Since the
idea of Miri's not returning was too horrible to think
about, she decided not to even worry about it. Or at
least that's what she told herself as she devoured the
cookies.

Kelly wasn't sure she would be able to make it
through the next minutes, and she almost fainted with
relief when, at nine and a half minutes, Miri started to
materialize in front of her. Only then did she realize
she should have had a camera to take pictures of
Miri's disappearance and return. Next time, she decided, weak with relief.

She waited until Miri was all the way back before
she ran over and hugged her. Miri half collapsed in
her arms, but then she pulled herself together.

"You smell of cookies," Miri whispered. "I want to
sit down right now."

So Kelly led Miri to the sofa. Miri sank into it and
put her hand to her forehead. "Boy, do I feel sick,"
she said. "Does it always make you feel that way?"

"I think you get used to it after a while," Kelly said.
"It's the short trips that really upset the stomach. Did
you eat the grapes?"

"There weren't any," Miri replied. "I went into the
kitchen and there were no grapes and for a moment I
panicked, like I had to eat grapes or else awful things
would happen, and then I realized it didn't matter

what I ate just as long as I ate something. So I ate some crackers. Then I walked back into the living room, and I switched channels just for a moment, and there was a documentary on channel 2, something about ostriches, I think, and I watched that for a minute, and then I turned back to *Margie Maclain*, and then I got all weird feeling again, and the next thing I knew things were dark and I was back here."

"Let's check in the *TV Guide* to see if there was a documentary on," Kelly said, and she ran over to the TV set to find the magazine. "There it is," she said. " 'Ostriches, Birds for Our Time.' You see, you changed history. If you hadn't gone back in time, you never would have eaten those crackers."

"If I hadn't gone back in time, you never would have eaten all those cookies," Miri pointed out. She sounded like herself again, Kelly was relieved to note. "I still feel sick to my stomach. How long does that last?"

"Only a minute or so," Kelly said. "I made notes while you were gone, too, so everybody'll know how brave you were to travel through time like that."

"Kelly, it's really significant what you've discovered," Miri said. "I didn't take you seriously before, but now that I've done it, I know how important it is. Maybe we can't save Abraham Lincoln's life, but there have got to be very important things you can do going back in time even just twenty-four hours. And we're just kids. I think it's time we let other people know."

"Not just yet," Kelly said. "For now, I think just the two of us should know."

"More than two know already," a voice said from up on the staircase. "Don't you know you can't keep secrets from me very long?"

⊚ CHAPTER 5

Scott Forrest awoke to the sound of his sister talking to someone in the living room. At first he thought he was dreaming, especially when he checked his clock and saw it was midnight. Kelly was weird, but she wasn't weird enough to be talking to herself in the middle of the night. Maybe in her bedroom she might have a little one-way conversation, but not in the living room.

That meant she was talking to someone, and even though it felt real nice being in bed, Scott was curious enough to force himself to get up.

He didn't put his slippers on, so he was quiet enough as he fumbled his way to the staircase. There was a good view of the living room from the middle of the stairs, and when Scott reached it he paused for a moment and looked down. There was Kelly all right, and she was talking to Miri. Scott shook his head in surprise. Miri was definitely not the sort of person to be hanging around other people's living rooms after midnight without a good reason.

Scott tried to make out what the two girls were saying, but it was hard at that distance, and the words he heard didn't make any sense at all. There was something about Abraham Lincoln and Margie Maclain and then a lot of discussion about apples and grapes. Kelly and Miri had some strange conversations, but this was the strangest Scott had ever tried to listen to. Whatever was going on, though, it was clear to Scott that Kelly was pushing Miri into doing something. That was nothing new. Kelly liked pushing people around. She did it to him all the time, saying it was her right because she was older than him. Two whole minutes older, but that was enough to satisfy Kel.

Then Kelly walked over to the VCR and began setting buttons. Scott watched carefully then, trying to figure out what was going on. It didn't look like Kelly was getting ready to watch a tape, but that was the only thing that made sense. Maybe Margie Maclain had starred in "The Life of Abraham Lincoln," and Kelly and Miri were sneaking around at midnight to watch it.

But then instead of Kelly's turning the TV set on, Miri walked over to the VCR. She looked like she was walking to the electric chair. Scott inched over quietly to get the best possible view of what was going on. Kelly could be weird on occasion, but Miri never was. Maybe Kelly had her hypnotized.

And then Miri pressed her hand on the VCR, and

right there, before Scott's unbelieving eyes, she disappeared. Not fast either, like maybe he blinked his eyes and in that quarter second she managed to climb out an opened window. But slowly, she faded from sight. There was a moment when Scott could have seen right through her. And then she was gone and he could hear Kelly say "Wow." Scott thought that was quite an understatement.

He waited for Kelly to shriek or call the police or do any of the things Scott would have done if his best friend had just turned transparent and disappeared. But Kelly stood still for a moment, and then she walked away from the TV set and went into the kitchen. Scott could definitely hear the sounds of Kelly opening the kitchen cabinets, ripping open a bag of cookies and devouring them. Kelly might not be very smart, he thought, but she knew in an emergency that eating cookies came after calling the police. So Kelly must not think it was an emergency that Miri had vanished.

Kelly was really going at the cookies, and there didn't seem to be much point in his standing on the staircase watching for her to go back into the living room. So Scott walked back upstairs and thought for a moment. Kelly wasn't big on diaries, but she was forever making notes about things. She claimed it was good experience for when she became an explorer, and her notes would be scientifically valuable. And she kept all her most important secret notes under her mattress. Scott had discovered that spot two years ago, when he'd helped his father turn all the mattresses over in the house and they found a whole stash of notes under Kelly's. Their father had thought it was cute, so he probably just told their mother and left it at that. But Scott checked under the mattress regularly to see if there was anything going on in Kelly's life he should know about.

So he tiptoed into Kelly's room, felt under the mattress, and came up with several sheets of paper. He took the notes and walked back to his own bedroom. He thought he could hear Kelly in the living room, but there was no sound of talking, so Miri couldn't be back. Assuming she ever was coming back. Maybe she'd disappeared for good. Kelly was going to have a lot of explaining to do if that was the case.

Scott took the notes and got under the blankets on his bed, with his flashlight conveniently placed to illuminate them. And then he read and learned all about Kelly's experiences traveling through time. At first he thought she was writing a story, but he knew his sister. The words had the ring of truth.

Scott couldn't believe Kelly's luck. There she was, playing with the VCR, exactly the way she wasn't supposed to, and she ended up traveling through time. What really made him mad was that Kelly seemed to think the best reason for traveling through time was to drink less milk at lunch.

But what Kelly had figured out, Scott realized, was that other people were going to have to travel, too, if she was going to get credit for it. So she must have convinced Miri to give it a shot, which was why Miri looked so somber when she walked over to the TV set.

Scott would be scared, too, if Kelly tried to convince him of something that harebrained. Except that it worked. At least it made people disappear, and that was pretty spectacular.

The question now was, was Miri going to be able to come back. Scott decided he'd better find out for himself, so he turned the flashlight off, got out of bed, and went downstairs again. He'd made a point lately of being as noisy as possible around people, so they wouldn't suspect that he could move as silently as a cat. Spying was a lot easier when people thought of you as noisy.

Kelly was writing in her notebook, he saw, and then she went back into the kitchen. Scott was tempted to go downstairs and read the rest of Kelly's notes, but in a moment she came back out of the kitchen carrying the bag of cookies with her. She sat cross-legged on the sofa, eating the cookies and checking the time. Scott figured Miri must be due to return pretty soon, and a good thing too. His legs were getting cramps from crouching.

But the waiting was worth it when Miri began to materialize in front of the TV set. It was the exact reverse of her disappearing act. First she was pale, and then she grew more and more solid-looking, until finally she was all Miri again, and Kelly ran over and hugged her, and then held Miri up as she half fainted in Kelly's arms. Scott felt an enormous sense of relief seeing Miri again.

She looked terrible, and Kelly helped her to the sofa. Scott didn't bother trying to hear them, since whatever they were saying couldn't be as important as what he'd found out for himself by reading Kelly's notes. Kelly got up at one point and checked something in the *TV Guide,* and for a moment Scott thought she was going to turn the TV on and watch a movie, but instead she and Miri talked some more.

Scott inched his way downstairs, convinced the girls wouldn't know he was there. He got close enough to hear Kelly say, "For now, I think just the two of us should know."

"More than two know already," he said from the staircase. "Don't you know you can't keep secrets from me very long?"

Scott loved the way they looked when they heard him. Kelly was more scared than she had been when Miri had disappeared before her very eyes. And Miri turned so pale, Scott was convinced she was going to faint.

"It's Scott," Kelly said when she turned around and saw him grinning at them. "Scott, how long have you been standing there?"

"Long enough," he replied, and walked down the rest of the stairs, joining them in the living room. "Long enough to see Miri disappear and reappear. Long enough to know Mom's going to kill you for eating all those cookies."

"I want a cookie," Miri said, and grabbed the bag from Kelly. "Scott, you have no idea what time travel does to your stomach."

"I can't wait to find out," Scott said. "Let's see, you

preset the machine for a certain time, and then you press the rewind button and hold on. That's it, right?"

"How did you find out?" Kelly asked. "It isn't in the manual. I checked."

"I have ways of finding things out," Scott declared. Kelly's notes were still under his covers. If she had half a brain, she'd check under her mattress as soon as she got upstairs. There was always a chance she didn't have half a brain, but Scott figured he'd better start giving Kelly credit. She was the one who had discovered how to time-travel, and even more important, tested it to make sure it wasn't just a fluke. "I read your notes," he told her. "You'd better change your hiding place. Everybody in the family knows about it."

"Oh great," Kelly said. "You're right. I can't keep anything secret around here."

"Kelly, we've got to figure out what we're going to do about this time-travel stuff," Miri said. "Your hiding place can wait. This is more important."

"Sure, you can say that," Kelly said. "You're not related to a family of snoops."

"Miri's right," Scott said. "Are you sure the three of us are the only ones who know about the VCR?"

"Of course," Kelly said. "Unless Mom and Dad look under my mattress on a regular basis also."

"They don't," Scott said. "Sometimes I put stuff there that might get you in trouble, just to check, and they never seem to notice. They've probably already forgotten."

"Well, it doesn't matter," Kelly said. "I'm still going to have to find a new place. Someplace sneaking little brothers of mine won't be able to discover."

"I am not your little brother!" Scott said.

"Will the two of you please stop?" Miri pleaded. "What matters now is that Kelly's figured out a way of traveling through time. We're not old enough to handle this by ourselves. We have to tell a grown-up."

"We can't just go around telling everybody," Kelly said. "Mom would kill me if hundreds of strangers started coming to our living room and playing with the VCR."

"They'd probably just take the VCR and give us a new one," Scott said. "One that doesn't let you travel through time."

"We don't know that the VCR will work this way anyplace but our living room," Kelly declared. "You want to tell Mom that the TV news crews are coming to photograph our living room before she gets a chance to buy new slipcovers? Thanks, but no thanks."

"Shouldn't we tell somebody though?" Miri said. "The FBI maybe, or the CIA? Or our senators?"

Scott shook his head. "Not until we know a lot more about it," he replied. "For starters, they aren't going to believe us. I wouldn't have, except I saw it happen. And you know Mom and Dad. They don't much like the FBI and the CIA. Dad says they all have files on him anyway, from when he was in college. They might think we were spies. I think we'd better do some more research before we tell anybody."

"What kind of research?" Kelly asked. "Or do you just want to time-travel yourself?"

"Of course I want to," Scott replied. "Both of you have. It's my turn now."

"It's too late tonight," Kelly declared. "Do it tomorrow, Scott."

"All right," Scott said. "Besides, that wasn't the kind of research I meant. We should find out if all VCRs can do this, or if it's just ours. I don't suppose you bothered to check that out, Kelly."

"I've known about this for only twenty-four hours," Kelly said angrily. "I've had other things on my mind."

"That's why it's good we all know now," Scott said. "Tomorrow after school, I'll see if Steve Leonard's machine lets you time-travel."

"You can't tell Steve!" Kelly cried. "He'll tell everybody at school."

"You're right," Scott said. "I'll do it without him knowing. I promise."

"I think we'd better help you," Miri said. "Whatever happens from now on, the three of us had better all be involved. Right, Kelly?"

Kelly bit her lip. "I guess explorers have to have sidekicks along," she said. "But just remember, when we tell the newspapers, I was the one who discovered it."

"Sure, Kelly," Scott said. It was like Kelly to want all the glory for herself, he thought.

"I've got to go home," Miri said, but as soon as she said it there was a soft knocking on the door.

"I don't believe this," Kelly muttered. She walked over to the door and whispered, "Who is it?"

"Pop."

So Kelly opened the door. Sure enough, there was Pop in his robe and pajamas.

"Hi, Pop," Kelly said. "What are you doing here?"

"I saw lights, I was worried," Pop said. "Is everybody all right?"

"We're fine," Scott said. "Keep it quiet though. Mom and Dad are still sleeping."

"We all should be sleeping, " Pop said. "It's way past midnight. Miri, what are you doing over here this time of night?"

"We were showing her the VCR," Kelly said. "Mom and Dad don't like it when we play with it, so the only chance we had to show it off to Miri was late at night."

"When I was a kid we sneaked smokes," Pop said. "Oh well, VCRs don't give you cancer. Come on, Miri. Let's go home so we can all get a decent night's sleep."

"Coming, Pop," Miri said. "Thanks for showing me everything," she said to Kelly and Scott.

"Anytime," Kelly replied.

"Anytime before midnight," Pop said. "Good night, kids. Sweet dreams."

"The sweetest," Scott said, and grinned thinking about all the exciting stuff he was going to have to dream about.

⊚ CHAPTER 6

"We don't really need three people for this mission," Scott declared the next afternoon as he, Kelly, and Miri stood in front of Steve Leonard's house. "Two will do just fine."

"Great," Kelly said. "You go home and Miri and I will handle it."

"I'm not leaving you to mess things up," Scott replied. "Why don't you go back to the house and work some more on your precious notes."

"Those notes are going to make scientific history!" Kelly shouted. "Without those notes, nobody's going to believe any of us."

"They'll believe it when they see it," Scott said. "And not because of any dumb notes you hide under your mattress."

"I'm not hiding anything else there ever again," Kelly declared. "Now that I've found out what a snoopy baby brother I have."

"Stop calling me your baby brother!" Scott yelled.

"Will the two of you stop it," Miri said. "One more word out of either of you, and I'm going to Pop's store to help him with the inventory."

"You can't do that," Kelly said hastily. "We need you."

"Fine," Miri said. "So stop acting like babies, both of you. I swear. You both say you're so worried about time travel falling into the wrong hands, and then you throw tantrums in public. I'd like to go back in time ten minutes and erase both of you."

"Wow," Kelly said. "Do you think we could be erased? I never thought about that."

"There's a lot you never thought about," Scott said. "No, I don't mean that as an insult. There just is. I made a list during English today of all the questions we need answers to, and that was one of them. Could we be erased? Could we go into the future by pressing fast forward? Would we still be able to time-travel if the VCR wasn't in our living room? Could more than one of us travel at the same time? Lots of things. We need more time to make our experiments and write our notes, and then we should tell the world."

"I still think we should tell a grown-up," Miri said. "One of our parents or somebody."

"If we told Mom or Dad, they'd be sure to trade in the VCR for a standard model," Kelly said. "I love Mom and Dad, but they lack imagination. And if we told your mother, then she'd just tell ours, and we'd be right back where we started."

"We could tell Pop," Miri suggested.

"Not yet," Scott said. "Maybe later. But right now we'd better see what we have, before we tell anybody else. Three people is already a lot to know about it."

"You were the third to find out," Kelly said. "You're no one to talk."

"That won't stop him," Miri said. "Or you either, I guess. Let's find Steve's machine and get this over with. I don't like any of this time-travel stuff, and the sooner we can tell other people, the better."

"It does unsettle the stomach," Kelly said. "But that's a small price to pay for the greatest invention of the twentieth century."

"That's what my mother calls her microwave," Miri said. "Let's not climb into that and see if it takes us anywhere, okay?"

"Okay," Kelly said, and giggled. "Now we all know what we're supposed to do."

"I'm going to grab Steve and try to talk him into throwing a surprise birthday party for the two of you," Miri said. "Except I don't know what to say if he remembers that your birthday is in April."

"Tell him it'll need a lot of advance planning," Kelly replied. "Meanwhile, Scott and I will be in his family room trying to travel back in time on his VCR."

"I'll finally get my turn to travel," Scott said. "You'll just be my witness."

"For five minutes," Kelly said. "Any more, and Miri might not be able to keep Steve in the kitchen. Five minutes, Scott, and that's it."

"I know," he grumbled. Kelly had been awful ever

since he interrupted her last night. She seemed to think she was the greatest thing ever because she had traveled through time twice and he had yet to do it. "Boys might not be able to," she'd even suggested as they'd walked to school that morning. Of course boys could, he thought, if they had the time to do it. But Kelly had seen to it that he'd never had a spare moment to try the machine out. It didn't help that Miri kept saying how awful it felt to do it. Miri always had a delicate stomach. Scott was sure he'd be great at time travel once he had the chance.

And now his chance was coming, and he didn't know if he wanted to succeed or not. On the one hand, even for five minutes, it would be great to go back in time. He'd selected his five minutes already, five minutes at school when he'd gotten an answer wrong to a question in math. He'd listened to the next kid give the right answer, so if he made it back there, he'd be able to give the right one and change history that way. It was at least as good as cartons of milk.

But if Scott did go back, it would be through Steve's machine, and that would mean VCRs let you time-travel, and that must mean Kelly wasn't the first one to find out about it. Not that he wanted Kelly splashed all over the front pages of the newspapers, looking smug and obnoxious. But he wanted their machine to be the special one, even if meant he had to postpone traveling through time for another hour or so.

"Be cool, everybody," Kelly said. "Let's not get Steve to thinking."

"Better none of us should think," Miri said, and she sounded so much like Pop, they all laughed. "Okay, I can handle it if you can."

"We all can," Kelly said. "Except maybe Scott."

Scott thought about killing Kelly right then. Could he go back in time and unkill her before he got into trouble? It was definitely an experiment worth trying soon.

"Just remember to keep your voices down," Miri said. "I'll have to whisper if I'm talking about a surprise party."

"We'll be quiet," Kelly promised. "Time travel isn't noisy."

"Fighting is," Miri pointed out.

"Let's get this over with already, okay?" Scott said, and he realized with a start that he was scared. It was one thing to talk about time travel, but it was a whole other thing to remember how Miri had looked when she'd been transparent. Kelly really didn't know what it was that she was doing.

On the other hand, if Steve's machine did let him time-travel, then it must mean lots of machines worked that way. Since Scott hadn't heard of people just vanishing, the odds were it was perfectly safe. In which case, Scott wouldn't mind at all that their machine wasn't special. And he certainly didn't want Kelly to see that it bothered him, so he made a big point of ringing the doorbell and looking as though nothing would ever bother him again. Steve finally opened the door.

"Hi, guys," Steve said. "What's up?"

"Nothing much," Kelly said, and Miri giggled. Scott could see Kelly give Miri a little kick to calm her down. "We just thought we'd visit."

"It was Miri's idea," Scott said. "She said she wanted to talk to you about something."

"Only we don't know what," Kelly said. "Miri wouldn't tell us. Would you, Miri?"

Miri giggled some more. "It's a secret," she said. "Something for Steve and me to talk about."

"Without us, I guess," Scott declared. "Can we come in, Steve?"

"Sure," Steve said, giving all of them strange looks. "What do you want to talk about, Miri?"

"It's kind of a secret," Miri said. "I told Kelly and Scott not to come along, but they insisted." She'd just made that part up, and Scott could see how proud she was of her creativity.

"Okay," Steve said. "Uh, where do you want to talk?"

"How about the kitchen?" Miri suggested. "Are your parents at home?"

"All alone," he said. "Joanie is playing with some friends of hers."

Joanie! Scott had forgotten that Steve had a sister. Thank goodness she wasn't there. They were just going to have to plan more carefully in the future.

"Great," Miri said. "Why don't you guys go watch some TV or something while Steve and I talk." She gave Kelly a little shove, and this time Scott grinned. Miri must have felt like shoving Kelly lots of times.

"We'll be in the family room," Kelly said. "Take

your time, Miri. Whatever it is you want to talk about."

"I will," Miri said. "I'll be very thorough. You guys be careful, okay."

"Why should they be careful?" Steve asked, but Miri was already leading him into his kitchen, so Scott didn't have the chance to hear Miri's explanation.

"Here's the VCR," Kelly whispered. "Oh good. It's the same kind Dad got for us."

"Of course it is," Scott said. "There was no point conducting this experiment on a different kind of machine. That's why I picked Steve's."

"So you did something right for a change," Kelly said. "Congratulations. Now let me set the VCR, and we'll see if we can get rid of you for five minutes."

"Why shouldn't I set it?" Scott asked.

"Because I'm the one who always sets it," Kelly replied. "You've never done it. How do you know you know how?"

"I know how," Scott said. "You just preset it and press the rewind button."

"You have to make sure there's no tape in there too," Kelly said. "See, Scott, you don't know how to do it. Let me."

"I knew about the tape," Scott grumbled. "Besides, you don't know for sure that that makes a difference."

"This isn't the time to find out," Kelly said. "One experiment at a time, all right? Now get out of my way while I preset."

"You don't know what time to preset it for," Scott pointed out.

"So tell me," Kelly said, her voice rising.

"Keep it down," Scott said. "We don't want Steve to hear us and come in."

"Sorry," Kelly said. "What time?"

"Make it 10:42 A.M.," Scott replied. "For five minutes. That's until 10:47, you know."

"I could have guessed," Kelly said. "I have enough fingers." She giggled, and Scott felt better. He didn't want Kelly to be so mad she might make a mistake with the machine and screw him up for good.

"Okay, it's all set," Kelly whispered. "Now hold on to the rewind button and don't let go. And be careful."

"I will be," Scott said. He walked over to the machine and, with a shaking hand, pressed the rewind button. Nothing happened. He held on to it a little harder, thinking maybe more pressure would make the difference, but he still was in Steve's family room, and there was Kelly looking puzzled, and the VCR wasn't doing a thing, and he felt pretty dumb just standing there.

"Let me try," Kelly said. "Get away, Scott."

Scott moved off. It would be worth it to see Kelly disappear.

Kelly pressed the rewind button and waited. Nothing happened.

"Are you sure you preset it right?" Scott asked.

"Positive," Kelly replied. "But I'll try it again, just to make sure."

"Do it fast," Scott said. "I don't know how much longer Miri can keep Steve in the kitchen."

"I'm doing it as fast as I can," Kelly said. "Okay. It's at 10:42 P.M. Go, Scott."

"I need 10:42 A.M," Scott said. "I was asleep at 10:42 P.M."

"What difference does it make?" Kelly asked. "I'll still watch you disappear, and we'll know if it works."

"It makes a big difference if you set the machine for 10:47 A.M. as my return time," Scott said. "You could end up standing here for twelve hours, trying to keep Steve in the kitchen the whole time."

"You're right," Kelly said, and she adjusted the machine. "Okay, it's set for A.M.," she declared. "Give it a shot, Scott."

So Scott went back to the VCR and pressed rewind. His stomach was so upset by all the tension, he didn't see how time travel could make him feel any worse. Again, nothing happened.

"Are you sure you set the machine when Miri went back?" Scott asked. "Maybe the person who's traveling has to be the one to set it."

Kelly shook her head. "I definitely set it," she replied. "And I did it right both times now. Scott, you just can't travel through Steve's machine. That's all there is to it. Our machine is special. They must have made a mistake with ours, and that's why it works and nobody else's does."

"We still don't know that ours is the only one that does," Scott said, but he suspected Kelly was right. And he was back to liking the idea. If they had the only time-travel VCR, it would be worth a lot more

money than if everybody's did. And they were the only ones who knew how to make it happen.

"Let's go rescue Miri," Kelly said. "Before we end up with a surprise party next April."

"I wouldn't mind a party," Scott replied. "Besides, if we don't like the party, we can always go back in time and make things better."

"I'll put it on my calendar," Kelly said. "Scott, just remember, Miri is right about one thing."

"Probably more than one," Scott said. "But what this time?"

"This time-travel stuff is serious," Kelly said. "It isn't a game."

That was easy enough for her to say, Scott thought, as he and Kelly walked into Steve's kitchen. She'd already had her fun with it, while all that had happened to him was to stand holding on to a rewind button. But no matter how Kelly tried to hog it for herself, Scott knew he was willing to risk everything to try time travel at least once for himself.

⊚ CHAPTER 7

Scott wasn't sure what the going price would be for a time-travel VCR, but he figured it would probably be a lot. Of course the machine had its limitations, like not being able to save Abraham Lincoln's life, but Kelly was right for once. If you were President and you did start World War Three and then changed your mind, the VCR would be a handy thing to own.

The only problem with selling the VCR, other than the fact that Scott had yet to travel through time, was that the machine didn't technically belong to him. Scott was willing to share the fortune with his family, even Miri, since she had been part of the experiment, but first he had to find out if his father would be willing to sell it.

So after supper that night, while Scott and his father were doing the dishes, Scott brought up the topic.

"You really like the VCR, don't you, Dad?" he began, drying each dish as his father handed it to him.

"Sure I do," his father replied. "When I was a kid I always dreamed of being able to watch my favorite TV shows over and over again. There were always reruns but I wanted something more than that. Of course old TV shows are to me what movies are to your mother. I used to love *Maverick* and *Have Gun Will Travel*. Great shows."

Scott nodded. "I like TV too," he said. "And I know what you mean about watching favorite shows over and over again. I guess I've seen *Star Trek* a hundred times."

"*Star Trek* first came on when I was in college," his father said. "We used to take time off from protesting the war to watch it." He smiled at the memory.

"But now with the VCR, you could tape it and still protest," Scott pointed out. "So I guess it is a great invention."

"Anything that gives you control is good," his father said. "And with the VCR you can control when you're going to watch your shows. Of course your mother thinks its sole purpose is to tape Humphrey Bogart movies." He chuckled. "I guess at some point we'll just have to get two machines, to satisfy both of us."

Scott's heart jumped. "Two machines," he said. "Do you think we might get another one soon?"

"Of course not," his father replied. "We just bought this one. We've hardly used it yet. Why should we run out to buy a second one?"

"I don't know," Scott mumbled. "It was your idea."

"Don't mumble," his father said.

"Sorry," Scott said. "I just thought, you know, maybe you'd get a second one right away, just in case the first one broke or something."

"Why should it break?" his father asked. "Have you and your sister been playing with the machine when you weren't supposed to?"

Scott shook his head. He wasn't sure if that was a lie, but he didn't think that what they'd been doing could really be called playing. Kelly sure wouldn't, not with her Nobel Prize at stake. "Things break," he said. "Or they don't work the way you think they're going to."

"That's true," his father said. "But I figure the VCR is good for a little while longer. The next one we get, it'll have all the video equipment so we can make home movies. Of course by then you and Kelly will be too old to do anything cute for the camera. Not that you do much cute stuff these days. You know, I can't remember the last time I looked at the two of you and thought, gee, what cute kids."

"That's good, Dad," Scott said. "Kelly and I are both too old to be cute."

"You're never too old for cute," his father said. "Be careful with those dishes, okay? Next investment I make is definitely going to be a dishwasher."

Scott nodded. "Dishwashers cost lots of money, don't they, Dad?" he asked. "More than we can afford, probably."

"They cost enough," his father said. "Why? Are

you thinking of dropping out of school and getting a full-time job just to buy us one? If you are, don't bother."

Scott laughed. "I think I'll stick around school a little while longer," he declared. "I still have some stuff to learn."

"I wish Kelly had your attitude," his father said. "I've never seen anybody so impatient in my life. Sometimes it worries me, how eager she is to grow up."

Scott paid careful attention to what his father was saying. He and Kelly had a deal that whenever one of their parents said something to them about the other, they'd report it back to their twin at the first opportunity. They both learned a lot of interesting stuff that way.

"What I meant about the dishwasher was maybe we could sell the VCR and buy a dishwasher with the money we got for it," Scott said, trying to sound casual about it.

"Why should we sell the VCR?" his father asked. "Scott, why do you keep asking questions about our getting rid of the VCR? Are you and Kelly fighting over it?"

"No, nothing like that," Scott said. "It's just, I thought maybe there were other things you'd like that we can't afford because you spent all your money on the VCR. Dishwashers. Trips to Europe. New cars."

"The VCR didn't cost that much," his father said. "How about giving me a chance to get tired of my new toy before we trade it in for a station wagon."

"Okay, Dad," Scott said. He took the dish his father handed him and began drying it. "I just was wondering how much money it would take for you to sell the VCR."

"I wouldn't sell it for anything less than what I paid for it," his father said. "And since the minute you take it out of the store, it becomes used, I would never get the money. So I guess we're stuck with it."

"But suppose somebody offered you a lot of money for it," Scott persisted. "Like a million dollars or something. Would you sell it then?"

His father stood still for a moment, thinking about it. "Not for a million," he said. "A million just isn't that much money anymore. It used to be, when I was a kid, but not with inflation. And we'd have to pay most of it out in taxes. So no, I don't think I'd bother selling it for only a million."

"How about a billion then?" Scott said. He didn't think they could get a billion for it, but you never knew. Maybe the Pentagon would want it, and according to his parents, the Pentagon always got what it wanted, regardless of how much it cost.

"Yeah, I'd sell it for a billion," his father said. "Actually, if somebody offered me even half a billion, I could probably be talked into it."

"Half a billion," Scott said. He wasn't sure just how much half a billion was, but it was obviously more than a million and less than a billion. It was good to know his father's price. The next question was how to tell the Pentagon the machine was available.

"Of course the only organization that would be willing to shell out half a billion for a VCR is the Pentagon," Scott's father said. "And I'm not sure I want to do business with them."

"Oh?" Scott said. He'd been having such a good time, too, trying to divide half a billion by five. It hadn't been easy, since he wasn't sure how many zeros were involved. "Why not?"

"You know how I feel about the military," his father said. "They'd probably take the VCR and use it to tape nothing but war movies or endless John Wayne Westerns. I'm not sure I'd like to see our poor VCR exploited that way."

Scott checked his father out carefully. He was definitely grinning. Scott decided to act like it was all a joke and laughed.

"John Wayne movies," his father said, shaking his head. "No VCR of mine is ever going to meet a fate like that."

"No," Scott said. "But what if the Pentagon could think of something else to do with the VCR. Something that didn't have anything to do with John Wayne. What then? Would you sell the VCR to the Pentagon if they weren't going to tape war movies with it? If they offered you half a billion. Or more even. Would you sell it then?"

"You're asking me about moral values, aren't you, son?" Scott's father said. "Wow. Your mother and I always said if we raised you kids right, you'd grow up aware of all the moral complexities of life. I guess what you want to know is, do I have a price? Is it true that everyone can be bought if they're offered the right price? That's it, isn't it, Scott?"

"Not exactly," Scott said. "I wasn't asking if you could be bought. Just if the VCR could be."

"Same thing," his father said. "I like to think that I can't be bought. I like to think that there are some issues I believe in so strongly that there's no amount of money big enough for me to sell my soul. And I hope that when you and Kelly are grown up, you'll feel the same way. Your beliefs are much more valuable than any amount of money could be."

"I'm not talking about selling your values," Scott said. "Just your VCR."

"But the VCR is a symbol," his father replied. "No, Scott. I don't think there's a price high enough for me to sell our VCR to the Pentagon so they can record John Wayne movies with it. And I hope that you can understand what I'm talking about, and that you'll respect my attitude and not try to convince me to do something I believe is wrong just for the sake of a few extra dollars."

"Half a billion is a lot more than a few extra dollars," Scott pointed out. This was getting sticky. His father might decide that the Pentagon wouldn't use the VCR to stop World War Three but to start it instead. And if he ever decided that, they'd never be able to do business.

"Millions for defense, but not one cent for tribute," Scott's father said. "When you get older you'll understand."

"I understand now," Scott grumbled. There he was,

sitting on the biggest invention since the wheel, and his father was getting all principled on him. It wasn't fair. Who was he supposed to sell the VCR to if his father wouldn't okay the deal with the Pentagon? Scott didn't think the American Civil Liberties Union would be able to afford it.

"This is great," his father said, handing Scott yet another dish to dry. Scott was sick of dish drying. A half a billion could pay for a lot of dishwashers. "Talking about ethics with my son. Not that I haven't enjoyed playing ball with you, teaching you my pickoff move to first and all, but when I was in college, and the world around me was going mad, I used to fantasize that I'd have a son I'd talk to about ethics. My father never talked to me about ethics. He didn't even have much of a pickoff move. And he certainly never did the dishes."

The more Scott learned about his grandfather, the more he liked him. Nothing against his father's pickoff move, but the three times Scott had tried it, he'd been called for balks. And he could live without the ethics.

"So even if the Pentagon offered a billion dollars, you still wouldn't sell them the VCR," Scott said. "Or even for two billion dollars."

" 'Fraid not," his father said. "We're stuck with it." He handed Scott the meat platter to dry, and Scott promptly dropped it. It smashed into five jagged pieces.

"Damn!" Scott cried.

"Scott," his father said. "You know we don't approve of your using language like that."

"What happened?" Scott's mother asked, rushing into the kitchen.

"I broke the damn meat platter," Scott said. "See."

"Scott, I just warned you about your language," his father said. "It's just a meat platter. It's not the end of the world."

"I bet you wouldn't sell it to the Pentagon either," Scott grumbled.

"Scott, if you had to break something, did it have to be the meat platter?" Scott's mother asked. "I don't know how I'll ever be able to replace it."

"If we sold the VCR to the Pentagon, you wouldn't have to worry about your damn meat platter," Scott shouted.

"That does it," his father said. "Three strikes and you're out. Go upstairs to your room, and when you're willing to talk without using profanity, you can join us."

"It isn't fair," Scott said. "It's all your fault, Dad."

"What's all his fault?" Scott's mother asked. "Scott, before you go upstairs, please sweep up the broken pieces."

"Sure, first I sweep and then I get punished," Scott said. "I bet you think that's real fair too."

"I have no idea why you're blaming me for any of this," his father said. "We were talking about ethics," he said to Scott's mother. "I guess Scott just has a different set from ours."

"My ethics are perfectly fine," Scott said. He went to the broom closet and got out the whisk broom and dustpan. "I have great ethics. I'd sell the VCR to the

Pentagon, that's all. I don't see why just because someone worries that they might use it to tape stupid John Wayne movies we can't sell it for a billion dollars."

Scott's mother shook her head. "I don't know why I even bother asking," she said. "I'm sure you and your father know why the Pentagon broke my meat platter for a billion dollars, but I don't and I never will. I don't even want to." She snorted and left the kitchen.

"I'm finished," Scott said, after throwing out the shattered plate.

"Fine," his father said. "Now go up to your room and think about what language is appropriate for an eleven-year-old and what isn't."

"I thought you believed in free speech," Scott said.

"Not for eleven-year-olds," his father said. "Jeez, I sound exactly like my father. Go upstairs. I'll finish the dishes myself."

Scott considered pointing out that they were finished, but there was no point. Anything he said would just get him into more trouble. As he walked through the living room he saw Kelly sitting on the sofa, reading a book and smirking. She loved it when he got in trouble. And this time she looked like she was enjoying it even more than usual.

That did it. Scott was going to have to figure out a way of selling the VCR for tens of billions of dollars and seeing to it that Kelly didn't get a single penny. Sure, she might have been the one to figure out how to use the machine, but he was the one who decided to sell it. And that was what counted, getting in touch with the Pentagon and selling the machine for so many billions of dollars that Scott would be able to afford his own country somewhere, far away from dumb fathers and stupid sisters.

⊚ CHAPTER 8

Scott lay on his bed and stared at the ceiling. It was amazing how bad things could turn out with hardly any work at all. The day had started so well last midnight, when he'd found out what Kelly was up to. But nothing had gone right ever since. He'd goofed up math, and Steve's machine didn't time-travel, so he still hadn't had a chance to try it out, and then his father had gotten all moral on him about selling the VCR, and he'd broken the dish, and just because he cursed he was sent upstairs like he was a baby, and he could hear Kelly giggling all evening long, enjoying every moment of his misery.

Scott was invited back downstairs less than half an hour after he'd been sent to his room, but he refused. It was all his father's fault, and he was so mad at him and his ethics that he was happier staying in his room avoiding looking at him.

The worst thing was that Scott knew he'd pinned his father in the corner, and that was why his father had developed such a dumb attitude about selling the VCR. If he'd only presented his argument better, then his father would be happy to sell the VCR, and they could all be rich together. And if that had happened, then Scott never would have broken the meat platter, and everybody would be happy. So Scott knew it was all his fault, and the thought drove him crazy.

He listened as, first, Kelly went to bed and then, an hour or so later, his parents did also. He was sure he could hear Kelly laughing at him in her room, but he wasn't about to go in there and make her shut up. He'd gotten into enough trouble for one evening.

Scott's light was off, and he tried to fall asleep, but he was too upset. Everything had gone wrong. The meat platter was just part of it, although he had the feeling he hadn't heard the last of it. But the mess he'd made of his talk with his father was the worst of it. There had to be a way of convincing him that it was in the best interests of humanity for them to sell the VCR for a billion dollars. All he needed was a second chance.

At which point Scott sat bolt upright. What was the point of time travel if not to give you a second chance? Sure, Kelly might waste her opportunities with drinking less milk, and she might even force Miri into eating crackers during her trip, but that didn't mean Scott couldn't use it for important stuff like talking his father into agreeing to sell the machine. Not to mention not breaking the platter.

Scott slipped out of his room. He could hear his father snoring, and the sound comforted him. What he was doing was for his father's own good. He'd like being rich once he got used to it. Scott never heard of anybody who didn't like being rich.

He went down into the living room and stared at the VCR. It looked harmless enough, sitting there, the digital clock announcing that it was 11:32 p.m. No one would ever suspect that it was capable of changing the history of the world, assuming Scott's father could be talked into letting it.

The machine seemed to have been preset. Probably one of Kelly's bright ideas, he thought, planning to get up in the middle of the night to mess around with time travel. He wouldn't mind so much if she had some idea of the importance of her discovery, but all she seemed to be interested in was getting people to eat. She had never once mentioned to him how much money they could get for the machine if they sold it to the right people.

There was a tape in the machine, too, so Scott figured Kelly was planning on an experiment to see if she could time-travel with a tape in there. It was just like her to plan another adventure and not consult with him about it. She wanted all the credit. Well, she wasn't going to get away with it. Scott was determined to time-travel on his own, without his sister bossing him around and telling him he was doing everything wrong.

He took the tape out of the machine and pressed the clear button, so whatever Kelly had preset the machine for no longer mattered. Then he guessed at what time he and his father had started talking about selling the VCR. He still wasn't sure what approach he should take with his father, but he knew the mistakes to avoid. And he would be especially careful when his father handed him the meat platter.

Scott set the machine for 7:25 P.M. and had it run for twenty minutes. Scott wouldn't need any more time than that to get his father to understand, once he'd actually time-traveled himself.

Scott knew what he had to do next. Just walk over and press rewind and hold on for dear life. If Kelly could do it, if cautious Miri could do it, then he certainly could. Just press the rewind button. Sure he'd evaporate, and his stomach would get upset, and there were no guarantees he'd ever materialize again, but the odds were he would. Everybody else had, after all. There was no reason to assume what worked for Miri and Kelly wouldn't work for him.

Unless maybe boys did time-travel differently from girls. Of course if that was true, Scott had better know before he began negotiating with the Pentagon. They might not like it as much if only the women generals got to go back in time.

Scott told himself he was being dumb. He could do whatever Miri and Kelly could do, and a lot more. He was just naturally a little scared, because he'd seen Miri turn transparent. That was the kind of sight that threw a person, at least a person with brains. Naturally, it wouldn't bother Kelly.

Scott closed his eyes and prayed that he would

come back safely without breaking the meat platter. Then he clenched his fists, opened his hands slowly, and pressed the rewind button with all his strength.

It was the most amazing sensation, unlike anything he'd ever felt before. At first it felt like he was flying, but then it was more like the world was moving all around him, but he was standing absolutely still. Then his stomach took a 360-degree turn, and it was all he could do to keep it inside his body. Scott looked fast to see if he could see himself disappear, but by the time he thought to look, it was already too late. He was standing in the kitchen, drying the dishes his father was handing to him.

"Why should we sell the VCR?" his father was asking. "Scott, why do you keep asking questions about our getting rid of the VCR? Are you and Kelly fighting over it?"

Oh no. He'd traveled back five minutes too late. He and his father were talking about selling the machine, and his father was already wondering about what was going on.

Scott tried to remember what he'd said before all that, so he'd know where he'd just come in to. Something about dishwashers, he thought, and how they should buy one.

"We're not fighting about it," he said, to buy some time. "Kelly and I both like the VCR."

"I assumed that," his father said. "The fights usually come when you both like the same thing, not when one of you likes it and the other one doesn't."

Scott tried to laugh. Time travel certainly felt

funny. Nobody had warned him about that, how light-headed he would feel, and how weird it was to know he was having a conversation he'd already botched up once.

"So what's the problem with the VCR?" his father asked.

"No problem," Scott said. "It's just that Kelly and I got into a discussion about it."

"You mean fight," his father said.

"Discussion," Scott said. "Over whether you'd ever sell the machine. She said you would, no matter who wanted to buy it. And I said no, you wouldn't sell it to just anybody. Like if the Pentagon wanted to buy it from you, you probably wouldn't sell it."

"That's an interesting question," his father said, holding a soapy dish in his hand. "Sure I'd sell the machine if the right people wanted it. And you're right, if people I didn't like wanted it, then the odds are I wouldn't sell."

Scott breathed a sign of relief. He'd just cut through ten minutes of perfectly useless ethics.

"That's what I said," he declared. "I said if you found out the VCR could be used for something noble and good, and people offered you lots of money for it, you'd sell it. Wouldn't you, Dad?"

"Noble and good and lots of money," his father said. "That's a hard combination to turn down."

"Wait until I tell Kelly," Scott said. This time-travel stuff was terrific. Next time he took a test, he was going to go home, check out what the right answers should be, and go back to take it over again. He'd be the only student in the history of the universe to graduate with a 100 average.

"So who's going to make this offer?" his father asked. "And why don't they just buy VCRs of their own and save themselves all that extra money?"

Scott shrugged his shoulders. "Just people," he said. "But I bet they'd be using the machine for noble and good reasons. They wouldn't do it just to tape old John Wayne movies with."

"I should hope not," his father said. "Well, let me know if anybody calls offering to buy the VCR for lots of money. But only if they want to use it for noble and good reasons."

"Okay, Dad," Scott said, and he decided to press his advantage. He might not have another chance this good again. "Dad, suppose somebody like the FBI or the Pentagon wanted to buy the VCR? Would you sell it then?"

"Never," his father said. "Next question."

"But suppose they were going to use it only for noble and good reasons," Scott suggested. "Like to prevent World War Three. Suppose the Pentagon called and said the only way they could prevent World War Three was if you sold them the VCR. Wouldn't you sell it to them?"

"I don't know," Scott's father replied. "I'm not sure I'd trust the Pentagon to stop World War Three. I think I'd rather keep the machine and stop the war myself instead."

"But suppose that's impossible," Scott said. "Only

the Pentagon can stop the war, and only with our VCR. Wouldn't you have to sell it to them then?"

"I don't have to do anything," his father said. "You know how I feel about the military. Let them buy their own VCR. I can tell them what store I bought mine at, and they can shop for themselves."

Scott couldn't believe how stubborn his father could be. He'd almost had him too. At least this time he'd agreed to sell the machine for noble and good reasons. The only problem was, his father would never think the Pentagon had any noble and good reasons. And only the Pentagon could afford the VCR if Scott held out for the billion dollars he was sure the machine was worth.

"Do you and Kelly talk about this sort of thing often?" Scott's father asked. "My ethical standards, I mean."

"All the time, Dad," Scott mumbled.

"Don't mumble," his father said. "I guess I'm flattered. I don't think I much cared what my father's ethical beliefs were when I was eleven. I just tried to keep out of his way as much as possible."

"I respect you a lot, Dad," Scott said. "And you know what I respect about you the most?"

"I'm scared to ask," his father replied. "My pickoff move, right?"

It was beyond Scott why his father was so proud of his pickoff move. "I like that a lot too," he said. "But what I'm proudest of is how open-minded you are."

"Thank you," Scott's father said. "I should be tape-

recording all this to play for you when you're a teen-
ager."

"I'm serious, Dad," Scott said. "You're a big
enough man to change his mind. When you're wrong,
I mean. Not that you're wrong very often. But if you
are, then you change your mind, and you sell the
VCR, even if it's to the Pentagon."

"I'm not that open-minded," his father said. "Be
careful with the meat platter, son."

"Sure, Dad," Scott said, but just knowing how careful he had to be made him tense up. Sure enough, as
soon as he got the dish in his wet hands, he dropped
it. This time when it broke, the pieces scattered all
over the kitchen. It looked like an explosion of meat
platter.

"Goddamn it!" Scott screamed. "I don't believe
it."

"Scott, you know better than to say that," his father
declared. "Now calm down, and start sweeping up the
pieces."

"What happened?" Scott's mother asked, running
into the room. "Oh no, not the meat platter."

"I dropped it," Scott said. "Do you mind? I
dropped your damn meat platter. So sue me."

"Don't you ever use that tone of voice to me, young
man," his mother said. "Now you sweep that mess up,
and go to your room, and think about what kind of an
apology you owe me."

"It was an accident," Scott cried. "I didn't mean to
drop your stupid platter."

"It wasn't a stupid platter until you dropped it," his

mother declared. "Clean it up and go to your room before I get really angry and forget that it was just an accident."

"It isn't fair," Scott said. "It's Dad's fault."

"And why is that?" his father asked.

The problem was, Scott couldn't remember. He knew it definitely had been his father's fault the last time around, but that was because of his father's stupid stubbornness. This time his father would have been just as stubborn, but then he hadn't had the chance. "I don't know," Scott mumbled. "It just is."

"Don't mumble," his mother said.

"Oh, I don't know," his father said. "It's an improvement over the whining and the cursing."

"I hate both of you!" Scott screamed. "Clean your own damn stupid plate!"

"That does it," his father said. "Upstairs right now. And don't even think about leaving your room until it's time for school tomorrow."

"I never want to see either of you again anyway," Scott said, and he ran out of the kitchen. It didn't help matters that Kelly was sitting in the living room with a huge grin making her look even uglier than usual. Scott wanted to ram the VCR down her throat. He stormed up the stairs, ran to his room, and slammed his door with as much force as he had left in him. He sat on his bed, screaming into his pillow for another few minutes until he felt himself get all light and woozy again, and before he knew it he was back in the living room holding on to the rewind button.

With no one around to hear him, Scott told the

VCR exactly what he thought about time travel. The machine didn't seem to care. Scott couldn't believe that he went back in time and actually made things worse. No wonder his father didn't want to sell the VCR to the Pentagon. It could be a dangerous weapon.

He went up to his bedroom, taking care not to wake anybody. With his current standing in the family, the last thing he needed was for his parents to find out he'd been playing with their stupid machine. He flopped down on his bed, and after an hour or so his stomach and his spirits settled down enough for him to fall asleep.

The next morning he went downstairs, deciding to talk as little as possible in an effort to keep out of more trouble. He apologized to his father, and was about to do the same with his mother when she stormed into the kitchen.

"All right," she said. "Who played with the VCR last night?"

"What do you mean?" Scott's father asked.

"I preset the machine to tape *Dark Victory,*" Scott's mother said. "*Dark Victory.* Bette Davis *and* Humphrey Bogart. And when I got up this morning, there was no *Dark Victory.*"

"Maybe you just set the machine wrong," Scott's father suggested. "Everyone says that happens a lot in the beginning."

"There was no tape in the machine," Scott's mother replied. "Somebody took the tape out, and I want to know who."

"I did, Mom," Kelly said. "Sorry."

"Sorry," her mother said. "Sorry. Of course you're sorry. Why did you do that?"

"I wasn't thinking," Kelly replied. "I woke up in the middle of the night really thirsty and when I walked past the VCR, I could see there was a tape in there, and I was sure you didn't mean to leave it in there, so I took it out. You should have told me you'd preset the machine. I never would have messed with it if I'd known. I really am sorry."

Scott stared at Kelly, who winked back at him.

"All right," her mother said. "But next time don't take it upon yourself, all right? And I will make a point of telling people when I've preset the machine."

"Good," Scott's father said. "I don't think I could handle another crisis so soon."

"That machine is nothing but crises," Scott's mother declared.

"You owe me one," Kelly mouthed at Scott when their parents' attention was focused elsewhere. Scott just nodded. He was going to have to start giving Kelly credit for a lot more brains than he ever suspected she had. Somewhere along the line she'd obviously slipped in some smartness lessons.

And the way Scott felt, he wouldn't mind a few lessons himself.

⊚ CHAPTER 9

Miri Weisberg took a bite out of her sandwich and put it down. "My mother's the only person I know who can mess up a tuna-salad sandwich," she declared. "One tablespoon of tuna for every three of mayo."

"Go back in time and make your own sandwich," Kelly suggested. "I thought you made them anyway."

"Usually," Miri said, and attempted another bite. "But this morning, Mom made sandwiches for all of us. Poor Pop."

"He probably likes it that way," Kelly said. "He probably gave your mother the recipe."

"Poor Mom then," Miri said, but she giggled. "Oh, here's Scott now."

"It took him long enough," Kelly said, but she moved over to make room for him.

Scott dropped his books and his lunch on the cafeteria table next to Kelly's things. "Did you start this meeting before I got here?" he asked.

"We wouldn't do that," Kelly said. "But next time, don't tempt us by being late. Okay?"

"Sorry," Scott said.

"We shouldn't be having meetings in the cafeteria anyway," Kelly declared. "Anyone could hear us here."

"And not understand a word we're saying," Miri said. "This is the only time that's good for all of us. I have to go to Pop's store after school today and help with inventory. Mom's threatened to dump me in an orphanage if I don't."

"All right," Kelly grumbled. "Scott, this meeting was your idea. Why don't you start? And whatever you do, don't say anything that people might understand."

Scott gave Kelly a withering look. "All I want to say is that this time-travel business is a lot more dangerous than I imagined."

"Don't call it that!" Kelly said sharply. "Call it . . . oh, I don't know. Call it medicine."

"Great," Scott said. "Then they'll think we're a drug ring."

"Baseball then," Kelly said. "We'll all call it baseball."

"That reminds me," Miri said. "I have softball practice tomorrow."

"Baseball," Scott said. "All right. This baseball business is more dangerous than I imagined."

Miri giggled. "I'm sorry," she said. "It sounds like Scott's George Steinbrenner."

Kelly ignored her. "Baseball isn't the least bit dangerous if you know what you're doing," she told Scott. "Of course if you insist on going back in . . . baseball without proper supervision, you have to expect to get into trouble."

"Scott went back too?" Miri asked. "Isn't it yucky?"

"It upset my stomach," Scott admitted. "But that wasn't the bad part. The bad part was I got into more trouble after I went back to fix up the trouble I'd gotten into the first time than I'd been in the first time, if you know what I mean."

Miri thought about it. "What kind of trouble?" she asked.

"Scott broke the meat platter," Kelly declared. "Twice." She grinned at the thought.

"What happened was I got so upset at myself for breaking the platter again that I lost control the second time," Scott said. "It's one thing to time-travel—"

"Play baseball," Kelly interrupted.

"It's one thing to play baseball when the only reason you're doing it is to drink less milk," Scott said. "It's another to do it so you can fix stuff up. I think Dad's right about not selling the VCR to the Pentagon."

"Wait a second," Kelly said. "You told Dad about the VCR?"

Scott shook his head. "Not the way you think," he said. "I just brought it up to see if he'd ever be willing to sell it. Theoretically speaking. I brought it up both times, and he wasn't willing to either time. Not even for a billion dollars."

"Do you really think you could get a billion dollars for it?" Miri asked. She wasn't sure just how much a billion dollars was, but she knew it was enough for all of them to retire forever.

"I don't know," Scott said. "Maybe just half a billion. But sure, we could get lots of money for it. A VCR like that, it's probably one of a kind. And there are a lot of things people could use it for, if they know what kind of trouble they could get into and use it carefully."

"There's more to baseball than just drinking less milk," Kelly declared. "It's a weapon, and it should be used only for good. Otherwise I might not get my Nobel Peace Price."

"I still say we've got to tell a grown-up," Miri declared. "Not somebody in the Pentagon. Just a grown-up who knows us and would know what to do with the VCR. Before we get into trouble ourselves and make a terrible mistake with the machine, and wind up erasing ourselves, or causing World War Three."

"Or break any more platters," Scott said. "I agree. Besides, the grown-up might know who we could sell it to, if Dad really refuses to let the Pentagon have it."

"Why not just tell your father?" Miri suggested. "You're going to have to tell him eventually, if he's going to sell it."

"Not Dad," Scott said. "Not yet. Someone he likes first, and then we can discuss it with him. Dad gets weird sometimes, when it comes to discussing large sums of money."

"Pop then," Miri said. "How about if I bring it up to him while we're doing inventory today?"

"It's fine with me," Scott said. "I'd feel better, too, if I knew a grown-up was involved."

"Just as long as he doesn't expect part of my Nobel Prizes," Kelly said. "I don't mind splitting the billion we'll get, but those Nobel Prizes are mine."

"Fair enough," Miri said. "I'll tell Pop that's one of the conditions."

"Do you think he'll listen to you?" Scott asked. "Grown-ups can be awfully close-minded sometimes."

Miri shrugged her shoulders. "Pop has an imagination," she said. "And he loves watching science shows on TV. So he might be willing to believe me."

"Otherwise we'll have to make him travel through time," Kelly said. "And that might be rough on older atoms."

"I'll see what I can do," Miri promised, and she took another bite of her sandwich to see if it had improved in the past five minutes. It hadn't. But it really wasn't worth that awful whooshy feeling just to go back in time and hide the mayo from Mom.

Miri thought about time travel after school that day as she walked to the store to help Pop. She really hated it. What she couldn't get over was that Kelly actually seemed to enjoy it. And even Scott, who had had a terrible experience, still wanted to try it again. Miri would have been just as happy never to go back in time again. Not that she could see any reason why she should have to. The Pentagon or whoever would want a demonstration, but Miri knew Kelly would be delighted to provide it. That was fine with her. Miri could still remember that sensation of turning transparent. Kelly hadn't warned her about that, just said she'd feel light-headed. Well, it was a lot worse than light-headed. It was light-bodied. And Miri had accidentally looked down while it was happening, and had seen right through her foot to the floor below. Just the memory of it made her sick to her stomach.

Miri knew she didn't have Kelly's sense of adventure or Scott's brain. That was fine with her. One of them had to be cautious and practical. Otherwise they'd forever be running off and getting into trouble. Miri kept the three of them in order. She also kept Kelly from killing Scott and vice versa. She served a purpose. She deserved part of the billion.

Pop was helping a customer when Miri got to the store. He smiled when he saw her and introduced her to the woman who was buying a newspaper, two magazines, and a package of sugar-free gum. The woman pretended to be interested in Miri's arrival, but she left as soon as Pop let her. Miri grinned. Pop could talk the ear off any customer he wanted, and the poor customer would never stand a chance. It was amazing he'd stayed in business as long as he had.

"Look what I got today," Pop said, and he led Miri to an opened box.

Miri looked in the box. "What are they?" she asked.

"Tins of sour balls," Pop replied, taking one out to show his granddaughter. "Aren't they beautiful?"

Miri examined the tin carefully. It looked English with old-fashioned wildflowers painted on it. "How many are there?" she asked. "Tins I mean."

"Two dozen," Pop said. "I'd forgotten I'd ordered them. They should sell well at Christmas."

"Pop, Mom wants you out of the shop by then," Miri said. "She wants you to sell stuff, not buy more."

"Your mother doesn't understand retailing," Pop declared. "She never did. No wonder she got that ridiculous job in consumer affairs."

"It isn't ridiculous," Miri said. "She helps customers who think they've been bilked. It's important work."

"And who looks out for the small businessman?" Pop asked. "We're the backbone of the nation, not that anybody cares."

"I care," Miri said, and kissed her grandfather on his cheek to prove it. "And the tins are lovely. Now how's the inventory going?"

"It's going, it's going," Pop grumbled. "A big job like that, you don't just get it done in one day, you know."

"I know," Miri said. "That's why I'm here to help. Do you want both of us to go in the back room, or should I stay out front in case a customer comes in?"

"We'll hear the customers," Pop declared. "I might as well have your company while I count. Come on back."

So Miri followed her grandfather into the back

room. It was lined with boxes of things, and had that
special sugary smell that she would always associate
with Pop.

He took one box off its shelf and began counting
the candy bars in it. After he reached twenty-three he
put the box back in disgust. "This is the most boring
job in the world," he declared. "You'd think computers could do this for us, and save human brain-
power for something more important."

"You don't have a computer," Miri pointed out.
"Besides, I don't think they can lift boxes up and
count things inside them yet."

"Someday, though," Pop declared. "Someday those
computers will be able to do anything. It'll be a golden
age then, when computers do all the drudge work and
we humans will be able to use our creativity for writing symphonies and painting great paintings. Just
think how much better Mozart's life would have been
if he'd owned a computer."

Miri wasn't sure just how much better it really
would have been, but she knew a golden opportunity
when she heard one. "Pop, do you think there are
machines being built now that can do things none of
us even dream of as possible?" she asked.

"You mean secret machines?" Pop asked, obviously
delighted to stop even pretending to do inventory.
"Machines the government knows about, but they're
not telling us?"

"Something like that," Miri said. "Or maybe they
got invented by mistake. Mutant machines."

Pop shrugged. "Could be," he said. "Lots of strange

things go on we don't know anything about. We're too busy with class-action suits against small businessmen for important things like mutant machines."

"Mom had to help with that suit," Miri said. "What kind of mutant machines do you think there might be, Pop?"

"Oh, I don't know," Pop said. "Maybe computers that are a thousand times smarter than the ones we've been told about. Computers that can lift boxes off of shelves and count what's in them for you. Computers that respect the small businessman, and appreciate what a life of sacrifice he has, just to see to it that the little guy has a place to buy his newspaper every day."

"Mom would be real happy if you sold your life of sacrifice," Miri declared. "You don't need a super-smart computer to know that."

"Your mother knows more than what's good for her," Pop said. "That happens sometimes when you make the wrong career choice. Your mother could have gone into retailing in a big way. She could have ended up head buyer for some big department-store chain. But no, she had to get a social conscience. We could all be on easy street if she'd just stuck to what she was good at."

"We could still all be on easy street," Miri said. "Pop, listen to me. What if I told you that Kelly and Scott have something in their house, a mutant machine, that could make all of us so rich, we'd be rich beyond anything we ever dreamed of."

"What are you talking about?" Pop asked. "Did

they invent a new program for a computer or something?"

Miri shook her head. "It has nothing to do with computers," she said. "At least not as we know them. I guess it's possible computers have something to do with it, but I don't know how. Of course I don't understand how any of it works, and frankly I don't want to, since the whole thing makes me sick to my stomach, but it is a very important discovery and we could all get real rich. Kelly said I could get rich, too, since I helped them out, but I guess that will depend on what her father says. Scott says it's fine with him too. There should be plenty of money for all of us if we sell it to the Pentagon."

"I'm glad one of us knows what you're talking about," Pop said. "You want to pass me that box over there, and I'll pretend to count what's inside it."

Miri handed Pop the box. "Listen to me," Miri said. "First of all, you have to swear to keep all this absolutely secret. If the information got into the wrong hands, who knows what terrible things might happen."

"I certainly don't," Pop said. "Look at this. Twenty-seven bars of Yummo Juniors. I couldn't give this junk away, it was so bad. You think your mother would help me sue the Yummo Company?"

"Pop, Kelly and Scott's VCR lets you travel through time," Miri declared. "For twenty-four hours. I did it once. I went back in time and ate some crackers. The *Margie Maclain Show* was on."

"I don't understand," Pop said. "You went back in time and ate crackers?"

Miri nodded. "Mom didn't have any grapes."

"Oh, of course," Pop said. "What would have happened if she'd had grapes? Would the *Margie Maclain Show* have gone off?"

"It isn't like that," Miri said. "Pop, it doesn't really matter what I did when I went back in time. What's important is that I did, and so did Kelly and Scott. Separately. We've all done it, and frankly it feels terrible, but still it's an awfully important invention, don't you think, and we could sell it to the Pentagon for a billion dollars, Scott thinks, and then we'd all be rich and you could sell the shop. What do you think?"

Pop tossed a Yummo Junior across the room. "I think you've been watching too much television," he said. "Miri, I appreciate that you're here to help with this inventory, and I certainly appreciate how you're telling me stories to help us pass the time of day, but next time tell me something a little more believable, all right? Mutant goldfish maybe. Giant goldfish that swallow fraternity boys. No more mutant machines."

"But, Pop," Miri protested.

"Start counting, Miri," Pop said. "Otherwise I'm going to have to start a class-action suit against you."

"You'll believe me someday," Miri said.

"Fine," Pop said. "And maybe there'll be a run on Yummo Juniors, and I'll make my fortune on them. Maybe the giant goldfish will want them." He laughed at the thought.

Miri looked at her grandfather. There would be no convincing him now, she knew. She'd just have to tell Kelly and Scott that the first grown-up she'd told the truth to thought she was crazy or lying or both.

⊚ CHAPTER **10**

"Strike three! You're out!"

Miri checked her watch as she stood at second base. It was already twenty after five. Her team was seven runs behind, and in one more out the game would be over, and she'd be able to go to the store and persuade Pop to go home early. At least that was her mother's plan for her that morning. Get Pop home early, so she could try to work on him one more time to sell the store. Miri grinned. She wished her mother better luck than she'd had trying to get Pop to believe in time travel. Pop was a man not easily convinced about anything he didn't care to believe in.

It occurred to Miri that if she tried stealing third, she might get thrown out and the game would end that much earlier. It was already the longest game she'd ever been involved with. It took a long time to reach a 29–22 score.

Still, if she got thrown out, she'd be the third out, and her coach might get angry. He might not, since Miri was sure he had better things to do with his time as well, but you never could tell. It probably wasn't worth the gamble.

Miri was right. Two pitches later, the kid at bat hit a bloop single, and Miri ended up scoring from second. She knew better than to ask if she could leave early. Her coach was fond of saying "The game isn't over until the last pitch is made" and stuff like that. Once the game started, you had to hang in there until the bitter end.

The bitter end took longer than Miri anticipated, as her team mounted a two-out rally and scored six more runs to tie the score. The coaches conferred, and it was agreed that the two teams would play one final inning. Miri noted that nobody bothered to ask either of the two squads about this. If the coaches wanted extra innings, then extra innings it would be.

So they played for a while longer. In the top of the tenth inning the other team scored five more runs, and even though in the bottom of the inning Miri's team gave it their best shot, they still ended up losing the game 34–29. Miri hoped her coach was satisfied.

She helped put the team's equipment away and listened while her coach reminded them that their fielding could stand some more work. It didn't matter. The championships were the following week, and that would end the organized softball season until next spring.

Finally, she was allowed to leave the playing field. It

was already later than her mother had hoped for when she'd given Miri instructions that morning. But Miri couldn't help it. Was it her fault the game went on forever? Nobody in the softball league could field, and that always meant long ball games.

She walked the fifteen minutes over to Pop's store and thought about all the homework she still had to do that evening. Kelly had suggested they all get together after everybody else was asleep and practice their time travel, but Miri had refused. So what if that meant she'd get a smaller share of the billion? She didn't see how they'd be able to sell the VCR anyway. Kelly's father didn't want to, and Pop refused to believe it could do anything special. So it wasn't like they could just call the Pentagon in the morning and cash the billion-dollar check that afternoon.

Besides, Miri was sure that once someone had traveled through time, they wouldn't want to do it again. And nobody would pay a billion dollars for a one-shot deal. Kelly and Scott were stuck with their VCR, no matter what that did to Kelly's Nobel Prize plans. Miri was going to get back to normal, do her homework, study for tests, help Pop with his inventory. Live as normal a life as she could knowing her two best friends were scrambling their atoms and becoming transparent for cheap thrills.

When she was a block away from the shop, Miri saw police cars. A barricade had been set up in front of Pop's shop. Miri began to run. There was no sign of a fire, so at least the shop hadn't been burned down, but something was wrong. She was terrified it had something to do with Pop.

"Don't go any farther," one of the policemen said to Miri as she tried to climb over the barricade. "This isn't a show for kids."

"What's happened?" Miri asked. "That's my grandfather's store. Is he okay?"

"Your grandfather?" the policeman asked.

Miri nodded. She could see two police officers in the store, and then she heard the sound of an ambulance racing down the street.

"Clear a path, clear a path," the policeman said as the ambulance came to a stop in front of the store. Two attendants came out with a stretcher.

"Pop!" Miri screamed.

One of the policemen came out of the store. "Doesn't look good," he said.

"Granddaughter," the other officer said, jerking his head at Miri.

"Listen to me, honey," the second officer said, taking Miri aside. "Your grandfather's been shot. There was a holdup, and the robber got away. We're taking your grandfather to the hospital right now, but it would help if we knew someone to call. Your grandmother, maybe."

"She's dead," Miri said. "You need my mother's number."

"Fine," the policeman said. "Give us your mother's number."

So Miri recited it. She only hoped her mother was home. The police officer left her and made the call.

While he was gone the ambulance attendants came out, carrying Pop on the stretcher. Miri tried to get closer, to see how he looked, but the first policeman restrained her. "Come with me," he said. "I'll drive you to the hospital. We'll get there the same time as the ambulance."

"Thank you," Miri mumbled. She couldn't believe any of this was happening. Pop had been fine this morning. He had gotten into a fight with her mother about selling the shop and he'd made giant-goldfish jokes and promised he wouldn't get home too late. How could any of this have happened? How could anybody shoot him?

"Pop never keeps much money in the store," Miri said as the policeman drove them to the hospital. "Why shoot him? Why shoot Pop?"

"Sometimes robbers get mad if there isn't much money," the policeman said. "Or maybe your grandfather refused to give him the money. We don't know just what happened. Nobody seems to have heard the shot. A customer came in and found your grandfather lying there, so he called the police. We got there only a few minutes ago ourselves."

"He'll be all right, don't you think?" Miri said. "He wasn't hurt really bad, was he?"

"I don't know, honey," the policeman said. "I'm not a doctor. We should all know better in a few minutes."

Miri kept quiet after that and stared out the window. For all she knew Pop was dead. She only hoped her mother would be at the hospital by the time she got there. Miri didn't think she could stand being alone any longer.

It took a few minutes for everybody to find everybody else, but by the time they did Miri's mother was indeed at the hospital. She was talking to a doctor in the emergency room. As soon as she saw Miri she ran over to her, and the two of them embraced.

"He's still alive," Miri's mother said. "But they have to operate. The bullet, it's in his chest somewhere. The X rays will show where, and then they'll remove it."

"Mom, is he going to live?" Miri asked.

"They don't know," her mother said. "All we can do is hope and pray and wait. Are you all right?"

"I'm okay," Miri said. "I just want Pop to be okay."

"We all do," her mother said. "Now listen to me, Miri. I'm going to have to call Uncle Bob and tell him what happened. He'll want to know, to come here right away. But that means leaving you alone. Will you be all right until I get back?"

"I will be," Miri promised.

"If you want, you can go to the Forrests and stay with them until this is all over with," her mother said. "You don't have to stay here."

"I want to," Miri said. "I don't want to leave you. Or Pop."

"All right," her mother said. "They're going to want us out of here. And Pop'll be taken into surgery in a few minutes anyway, so we'll do most of our waiting someplace else. Let's find out where we should go, and then I'll call Bob from there."

Miri took her mother's hand and felt them both
shaking all over. They walked together to the main
waiting room, and after Miri sat down her mother
found a pay phone and made the call.

And then they sat and waited. Miri had never
known time could pass so slowly. There was nothing
to do but sit. After a while Miri got up and asked her
mother if she could call Kelly.

"That's a good idea," her mother said. "It might be
on the radio anyway. Call them and tell them we'll be
sure to let them know as soon as there's news."

So Miri made the call. Kelly's mother answered the
phone, and Miri told her about the shooting.

"I'll be right over," Kelly's mother declared. "Tell
your mother I'm on my way."

"All right," Miri said, and hung up. When she told
her mother she just smiled. "That's nice," she said,
but Miri wasn't even sure her mother had heard her.
She looked at her watch again.

"I just wish I knew how long the surgery was supposed to take," she said to Miri. "Twenty minutes.
Five hours. I have no idea. Do you?"

Miri shook her head. "They never taught us that in
school," she said. "How long it should take."

"No, of course not," her mother said. "I don't even
know why I asked."

"When's Uncle Bob's flight getting in?" Miri
asked.

"I don't know," her mother said. "It'll take awhile
though, even if he can make great connections. By the
time he gets here, this should all be over. The surgery,

I mean. He'll probably get mad at me for making him come. And Pop. Pop'll be furious that I called Bob away from his precious work."

Miri tried to smile. Uncle Bob managed a chain of bookstores. Pop always held that up to Miri's mother as the proper choice of careers for the child of a small businessman. "No class-action suits there," Pop used to say. Miri prayed he would say it again.

Kelly's mother arrived a few minutes later. "Any news?" she asked as soon as she found Miri and her mother sitting on the waiting-room sofa.

Miri's mother shook her head. "They've been in there for over an hour," she said. "Kate, I'm worried sick."

"That's a good sign though," Kate Forrest said. "Over an hour. I mean, if the bullet had done too much damage, then the surgery would be over sooner."

"What you're saying is, if he died, it would be over with already," Miri's mother said. "I know. That's what I keep telling myself."

"He can't die," Miri said.

"He won't die," Kate said. "Pop is one tough bird. It'd take more than a bullet to stop him."

"Not while he's working on his inventory," Miri's mother said, and half laughed. But then she started to cry. Miri was grateful that Kate was there to hold her. Miri didn't think she had much comfort in her to offer.

They'd been waiting close to two hours before a doctor finally came out. "Mrs. Weisberg?" the doctor asked, and Miri's mother immediately got up and walked over to him. Miri and Kate followed.

"We were able to remove the bullet," the doctor said. "It wasn't easy, because it hit a bone and shattered, so there were a lot of pieces."

"That doesn't sound good," Miri's mother said.

"It isn't," the doctor said. "One of the pieces hit the heart."

Miri's mother clenched her fists. "Is he still alive?" she asked.

The doctor nodded. "The next twelve hours are critical," he said. "I'm afraid it could go either way. Your father is not a young man, but he seems to be in good physical condition. And he's clearly a fighter. So we have that going for us."

"He can't die," Miri said. "I won't let him."

The doctor smiled at her. "That's the spirit," he said. "Believe me, we're doing everything in our power to see to it that he'll make it through this."

"You don't understand," Miri said. "I won't let him. I won't."

"Miri," her mother said.

"Kate, take me home," Miri said. "To your house. Right now, okay?"

"Will you be all right alone for a few minutes?" Kate asked Miri's mother.

"Sure," she said. "Get Miri home. Then come back here, if you don't mind."

"You couldn't keep me away," Kate said, and gave Miri's mother a hug. "Come on, kid," she said to Miri. "We'll get you out of here right now."

"I won't let him die," Miri told her.

"I know," Kate said. "And neither will the doctors. Pop's going to pull through this just fine. I know it too."

There was no point explaining. Miri didn't think Kate was ready then to hear about time travel. But she knew if she could just go back in time, she could prevent the whole thing and Pop would be fine. Miri didn't know how she'd do it, but she knew she had to try. Pop's life might depend on it.

Kate dropped her off in front of the house and watched as Miri walked in. Then she turned the car around and drove back to the hospital. Miri was glad her mother wouldn't be alone. Of course soon it wouldn't matter. Soon she'd be back in time, getting Pop out of the store, back to his home, before any stupid robber came with a gun to shoot him.

Kelly and Scott were waiting for her the minute she got in. "Where's your father?" Miri asked.

"He's in the kitchen," Kelly said. "Making supper. Do you want to talk to him?"

"I want him to stay in the kitchen," Miri said. "I have to travel back in time and get Pop out of the store before any of this happens."

"Do you know when he was shot?" Scott asked. "We need to know the time to set the machine for."

Miri shook her head. "I was playing softball at twenty after five," she said. "But the game went on for almost a half hour after that. And then I had to walk to the shop. I don't think Pop could have been lying there for very long before then. Lots of people come in after work, so somebody should have found him pretty soon."

"Do you really think you should go back?" Kelly asked. "It could be dangerous, Miri. The robber could shoot you too. Or even if he doesn't, if you do something wrong, then he could kill Pop. The way it happened with Scott when just being there knowing what was going to happen made things worse."

"I have to take that chance," Miri said. "Pop could be dying right now. And I don't think we should use the machine to make people come back to life again, even if it could do that. So I've got to act fast, and I've got to take the chance."

"You want me to go instead?" Scott asked.

Miri shook her head. "I'll do it," she said. "Just help me get back in time to twenty after five. I don't know what I'll do, but I'll figure it out once I'm there. I'll do anything I have to to save Pop's life."

"I'll set the machine," Kelly said. "Scott, you see to it that Dad stays in the kitchen. I don't think I could take explaining things to him now."

Scott nodded. "Miri, be careful," he said. "Maybe you should call the police when you get back in time."

"To tell them Pop's going to get shot?" Miri replied. "I don't think that'll work. Don't worry, Scott. I'll know what to do when I have to."

Scott nodded. "We'll be waiting for you," he said. "Do what you have to."

"I will," Miri promised. "Come on, Kelly. Let's get me back there before it's too late!"

⊚ CHAPTER 11

It was 5:20 P.M. and there were two outs as Miri stood on second base. The next batter up was going to get a bloop single and force the game to go another half hour unless she did something fast.

So Miri stole third. She ran as slowly as she possibly could without looking ridiculous, but the catcher threw the ball wildly to third base, and the ball ended up in left field. Miri naturally made it to third before the ball, and the umpire called her safe.

"No I'm not," Miri protested, even as the third baseman bumped into the left fielder in an effort to get the ball back to the infield.

"Of course you are," the umpire replied. "You can try to score if you want."

That was the last thing Miri wanted. While she might possibly have changed fate enough that her team would fail to tie the game, she didn't want to take that chance. "Interference," she said, digging the word out from the back of her brain. "I interfered."

"How?" the umpire asked.

"It's kind of hard to explain," Miri said, trying hard not to look at her watch. "But I did. I interfered with the catcher's line of vision." She looked dejectedly toward the ground. "So you really should call me out for interference."

"But that would end the game," the umpire pointed out. "And your team would lose."

"I know," Miri said, knowing no matter what happened, her team was going to lose. "But it isn't whether you win or lose, it's how you play the game. And I wouldn't want it on my conscience if my team won just because I cheated. I didn't mean to, but I did, and when a base runner interferes, then she's out. Right?"

"Right," the umpire said.

"What's going on?" Miri's team manager asked, coming over to third base.

"She interfered," the umpire told her. "So she's out, and the game's over." The umpire made the out sign finally, to emphasize the point.

"What do you mean the game's over?" the manager asked, but Miri didn't care how long the discussion went on. She ran toward home plate, grabbed a baseball bat that had been left on the ground while everybody stopped to watch her discussion with the umpire, and began sprinting out of the playing field and onto the street.

"Bring back that bat!" the manager called. "M ri, that's team equipment."

"Sorry," Miri shouted back, and kept on running. It was the closest thing to a weapon she'd been able to think of. With luck, she wasn't going to need a weapon, except maybe to threaten Pop with, to get him out of the store. But Miri felt better knowing she had something with her, just in case.

She was already three blocks away from the playing field when she remembered that she'd left her jacket and books behind. For a moment she stood absolutely still and couldn't think what to do. Part of her wanted to keep on running, to make sure she got to Pop before the robber broke in. But she also knew that if she did get Pop out of the store unharmed, she was going to have to explain not only why she had stolen a bat, but what had become of her books and jacket. And if they turned up missing the next day, Miri was going to be in lot of trouble. Making funny noises about time travel and saving people's lives wasn't going to get her out of it.

So she turned around and ran back to the playing field. Her team's manager was standing there all alone.

"I was wondering if you were planning on coming back," the manager said. "You have a lot of explaining to do, Miri."

"I know," Miri said, although what she didn't know was how she was going to explain any of it.

"First of all, why did you say you'd interfered when you obviously hadn't?" the manager said. "Why did you deliberately get yourself called out, and end the game, and ruin everybody's fun?"

"I had to go to the bathroom," Miri improvised. "So bad that I thought I would die if I had to stay here any longer. We've been playing for such a long time, and I had to go so bad, and I couldn't figure any other way. And we were so far behind, and there were two outs anyway, that I didn't think anybody else would really mind if I ended the game that way."

"It wasn't fair to the other players," the manager said. "If you weren't feeling well, you could just have asked for another kid to run for you and left the game."

"I could have, couldn't I?" Miri said. "I forgot that. Next time I'll remember. Thanks, Mrs. Dale."

"All right," the manager said. "So now we know why you threw the game. Why did you steal the bat?"

Miri looked at her watch. All this was valuable time she could spend rescuing Pop. "I needed it," she said. "I'll bring it back tomorrow, honest."

"You know better than to steal equipment," Mrs. Dale said.

Miri nodded. "But I have to have it," she said. "You know how sometimes you just know things, and you don't quite know how you know them?"

"Maybe," Mrs. Dale said.

"Well, that's how I know I have to have the bat," Miri said. Scott, she knew, would have come up with a better story than that, but he wasn't there to help. "I'll return it tomorrow, honest. Now if I can have my jacket and books, I'll get out of here."

"I expect to see that bat tomorrow immediately after school," Mrs. Dale declared. "In one piece too."

"It will be," Miri said, grabbing her books and jacket. "Thanks for being so understanding, Mrs. Dale. Next time, I promise I won't interfere."

"You'd better not," Mrs. Dale said. Miri jogged off the field, trying to look casual. As soon as she reached the street she began to run.

She ran all the way there and cut close to seven minutes off the trip. Everything looked just the same as it had the first time, she noticed as she ran. Nobody knew how the world had changed and what she was planning to do to change it back. All the stomach sickness, and that horrible transparent feeling, all of it was worth it if she could just save Pop.

She ran almost into the doorway of the store, but then she slowed down. For all she knew the robber was in there already. But a quick look in showed Pop reading a magazine. In spite of herself, Miri grinned.

"Hi, Pop," she said, walking into the store. "I'm here to take you home."

"What are you talking about, home?" Pop replied. "It's hardly 5:30. Way too early for me to close up."

"Mom wants us both home early for supper tonight," Miri told him.

"So she can get on me some more about the inventory," Pop grumbled. "Your mother thinks she understands about retailing. She understands nothing. Inventory's just the kind of job you can't rush. You do it too fast, you lose count, everything gets messed up, you have to start all over again. Haste makes waste."

"Don't tell me, tell Mom," Miri said, grabbing Pop by the arm. "She'll be happy to hear all about it."

"Miri, please," Pop said, wresting his arm from her grip. "Don't be rude. I owe it to my customers to stay here until 6:00. A lot of them, they come in after work, they want to buy a paper, maybe a candy bar for the kids, say good evening to me. It's part of the job. I can't leave now, no matter what your mother says."

"They won't mind for just one night," Miri said, trying to keep the desperation out of her voice. Did she dare tell Pop about the time travel? He hadn't believed her the first time; she might do more damage by bringing it up. And she didn't know what the time-travel rules were. She knew that was because there were no rules, but knowing that didn't make her feel any better.

"Five more minutes then," she pleaded. "And then you have to come home, Pop. Honest. I promised Mom I'd get you home early. I don't know what she wants to talk to you about, but it must be something important. And you know how Mom gets when you keep her waiting."

"She's my daughter, not my mother," Pop said. "She can wait for me once in a while. It won't kill her. I'm leaving at 6:00 and not a minute sooner."

Miri licked her lips. She'd known Pop's stubborn streak might show up, but she hadn't been able to come up with a way of getting him to move if it did. There had been so little time to make plans. Miri only wished she knew what time the robber was going to come.

"How's this for a compromise?" she said. "We stay here for another ten minutes or so, and you use the time to do inventory. I'll stay out front in case there are any customers. Then if Mom gets upset, at least we can tell her you were working on the inventory and that's why it took us so long."

Pop sighed. "Call me if you need me," he said.

"Sure," Miri said. "Don't worry about a thing. Just go back there and count."

"I hate inventory," Pop declared.

"I know that, Pop," Miri said, but she felt better as she watched him walk into the back room.

With Pop in the back room, there was at least a certain measure of safety. If she got him to leave in ten minutes, they might miss the robber anyway. Or if the robber came while Pop was in the back, he might not rob the store. Miri tried to look threatening as she stood behind the counter, her baseball bat by her side.

Of course Miri was also aware that she increased the risk to herself by being out in the front of the store, where the robber might shoot her. But she didn't see that she had a choice in the matter. And as long as she was prepared for the robber and he didn't take her by surprise, the way he must have taken Pop, she had a better chance against him. At least that's what she told herself as she stood there praying Pop would change his mind and agree to leave the store early and save both their lives.

Pop was right about the early evening customers. Miri kept fairly busy as people came in to make purchases. Occasionally Pop would call from the back room to see if Miri needed his help, but each time Miri told him to stay there and count. What she didn't tell him was how her heart leapt as each customer opened the door. Was this one the robber? she asked herself as one innocent person after another walked in, bought something, made small talk, and left. It was the longest, most terrifying ten minutes of Miri's life.

But finally the ten minutes passed. "Come on, Pop, time to close up," Miri called to the back room. "Let's not keep Mom waiting any longer."

"I'm counting," Pop said. "Another two boxes, and then I'll be finished with this section."

Miri couldn't believe it. All this time Pop had been dragging his feet over the inventory, and now, when she needed him to leave, he decided to get into it. "Now, Pop," she said. "The boxes can wait."

"Five more minutes," he said. "Then I'll have some good news for your mother when she asks."

Miri looked at her watch. If only she knew when the robber was going to come. Or if he was going to come at all. Maybe just by being in the store she'd changed history enough that he wouldn't show. She couldn't wait until they sold the machine to the Pentagon and let them run all the experiments to figure out just how time travel worked. At this point she would have happily given them the VCR, once she was finished with rescuing Pop.

"Now, Pop!" she called to the back.

"Now," he grumbled. "All right. That last box will wait if you're so impatient to get home. But it's on your conscience when your mother complains."

"Fine," Miri said. She took the baseball bat and walked away from the counter to the back of the store, where she'd flung her jacket and schoolbooks when she came in. She had a special spot behind the shelves for her stuff when she was too lazy to put things in the back room.

Pop walked over to the cash register to take that day's money out. And as he did the robber came in.

Miri froze. Then she ducked behind the shelf. She didn't dare scream for fear the robber would start shooting.

"Gimme your money, old man," the robber said. He had a ski mask over his face, and he was holding a gun, which he pointed straight at Pop.

"Get a job," Pop said almost conversationally. "You want to help me with the inventory, I'll be glad to pay you. No work, no money."

"You don't seem to understand," the robber said. "This is a gun, old man, and it's loaded. Now give me your money before I have to use it on you."

Pop stood still for a moment, and then Miri realized what he was thinking. If he had been all alone, he probably would have kept on harassing the robber. But he had just remembered that Miri was in the store, too, somewhere, and he wasn't about to take any chances.

Should she? Pop began to hand the money over to

the robber. If the robber just left, Pop wouldn't be hurt, and neither one of them would be risking their lives. She stayed absolutely still, trying hard not to breathe, as Pop gave the robber the money.

The robber checked the money out with his free hand. "This all?" he asked. "Don't hold out on me, old man."

"I'm not," Pop said, and Miri could see he was scared. "That's all I've got, honest. You want more money, go rob a bank."

"Don't tell me what to rob, old man," the robber said. "You have more money stashed in the cash register. Hand it over to me."

"I've given you all I have," Pop said. "Honest. I swear it."

"Now!" the robber screamed, and he cocked his gun.

That did it. Miri couldn't wait to see if it would all turn out peacefully. She grabbed one of the tins of sour balls and tossed it through the window. The window smashed with a gratifying noise.

The robber turned around to see what had caused the noise. Miri ran out from behind the shelf and set herself to swing the bat with all the strength she had.

But as she prepared to swing she heard Pop shout, "Miri, no!" And the whooshy feeling hit her at the same time, and she could feel the strength ebbing away from her. It was all a matter of seconds, but it felt more like an eternity.

Miri willed herself to stay in that time for just five more seconds. She swung the bat, and thought she

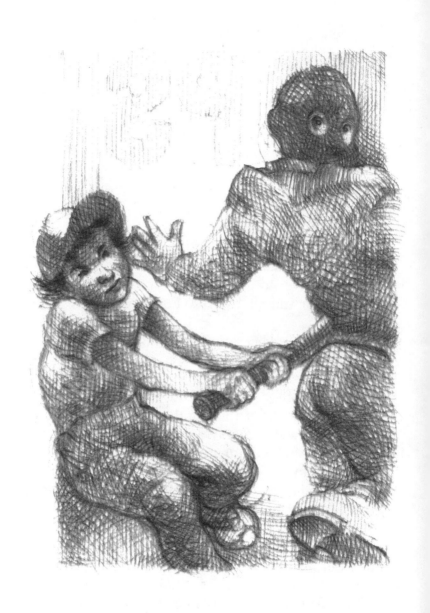

could feel it hit against flesh, but she could no longer be sure what it was she heard and felt. There was a floating sensation, and as she felt herself flying back she heard the sound of the gun going off.

⊚ CHAPTER 12

"No," Miri screamed, as she felt herself turning back into herself in front of the Forrest family's VCR. "No!"

"Miri, it's okay," Kelly said, grabbing her before she fell. "Miri, you're back here, and it's okay."

Miri shook her head, and then she felt her legs lose all their strength. She sank onto the floor, and for a moment all she was aware of was darkness. It occurred to her as she lost consciousness that the robber's bullet might have hit her. Maybe she was dead, she thought. Someone splashed cold water on her face, and she came back to life with a start.

"Sorry," Scott said. "It was Kelly's idea."

Miri managed to sit up. "Pop?" she asked.

"He's fine," Kelly said. "He's fine, and you're a heroine, and you'd better get in shape pretty soon because your family is worried sick about you, and everybody wants to know where you are."

"There was a shot," Miri said. "I swung the bat, and there was a shot."

"It hit the wall," Scott told her. "And when you broke the window a half a dozen people on the block called the cops. Nobody knew what became of you, but otherwise everything is fine."

"I don't understand," Miri said. "I feel terrible. Kelly, I really think I'm allergic to time travel."

"You'll never have to do it again if you don't want," Kelly promised her. "Listen, Miri, and listen fast. You hit the robber with the baseball bat."

"Right in his kidneys," Scott said. "They had to take him to the hospital."

"Oh no," Miri said. "I never meant to hurt him."

"Miri, he deserved it," Kelly pointed out. "He was pulling the trigger when you whacked him. Anyway, in the confusion, you left the shop. Everybody wondered where you'd gone to, so we just said you had probably gone off to calm down and that you'd turn up here eventually. Which, of course, you just did."

"I'm so confused," Miri said. "The time. Where did all that time go?"

"We don't know," Scott said. "I don't think we'll ever know."

"We'll find out eventually," Kelly declared. "Anyway, it doesn't matter now. What matters is that Pop is just fine, and you've got to act like what happened the second time was the only thing that happened. Things are confused enough without us breaking the story of time travel to the world this evening."

"The newspapers want to interview you," Scott

said. "And the radio station. You know. Kid saves grandfather's life. The police need to talk to you too."

"I'm going to be very sick," Miri said, and she ran to the bathroom.

"She's here, Mom!" she heard Kelly call out, and Miri was even gladder of the few minutes of protection being sick in the bathroom was providing her. She didn't know what she was going to face when she had to talk with everybody.

She stayed behind the bathroom door for as long as she dared, and then she left to join the others. All four Forrests were in their living room, as were Miri's mother and Pop. They all looked worried, and Miri didn't blame them.

"Are you all right?" her mother asked, embracing Miri. "We were so scared when you vanished like that."

"I just needed time to think," Miri said. "I don't know what I needed, really. I just walked around for a while, I guess, until I felt well enough to come back here."

"But why didn't you come home?" her mother asked. "Why come here instead?"

Miri managed a small smile. "I knew I was going to throw up," she said. "Why get sick at home when you can do it next door?"

Everybody laughed. "Our bathroom is your bathroom," Kate Forrest declared. "And since you're all over here anyway, why don't I make supper for all of us?"

"Thank you," Miri's mother said. "With every-

thing that's been going on, I haven't even thought
about supper."

"I'm famished," Kelly said. "What are we having
for supper, Mom?"

"Pizza," Kate replied. "Will pizza bother your
stomach, Miri?"

"I'm fine now," Miri assured her. "Pop, are you
sure you're okay?"

"Couldn't be better," he declared. "Now that
you're back, and I can see you're all right too."

"I'm just fine," Miri said, and to her surprise, she
realized that was true. She felt solid again, and happier
than she had ever dreamed possible. Proud too. She'd
set a mission for herself, and she had accomplished it.
She grinned at Pop. "Next time, go home when I tell
you to," she said.

Pop grinned back. "Next time, I will," he said.

Miri wasn't sure how she got through the rest of the
evening. Her mother and grandfather made an enormous fuss over her, checking her out to make sure she
hadn't been hurt, that she was still sane, that she knew
what had happened and that she could handle it.

"I'm fine," she kept telling them.

"How did you think to throw that tin?" her mother
asked between worried looks and slices of pizza. "I
never would have thought so fast. I'm afraid I would
have just fainted."

Miri shook her head. "You would have done just
what I did," she said, and then she grinned. "I just
remembered," she said. "Before I threw the tin, I

thought of Kelly. I guess I did what I figured she would do."

Everybody laughed, Kelly included.

"It was still fast thinking," Kelly's father declared. "I've always said you're the one I'd want with me in an emergency, Miri."

"I thought you said you'd trust her to operate on you, Dad," Kelly declared.

"That too," he said. "Miri is a remarkable young lady."

"No I'm not," Miri said, although at that moment she did indeed feel remarkable. "I just did what I had to, to save Pop. After all, if he'd gotten shot, he never would have finished his inventory."

"Forget the inventory," Miri's mother declared. "That store has got to go, Pop, while we're all still alive."

"We'll argue about that later," Pop said. "Right now let's just be grateful the only one of us feeling any pain is that stupid robber."

"I really whacked him, didn't I?" Miri said. "That was the best swing I've ever taken."

"You sure didn't step into the bucket," Scott said, and everybody laughed some more.

"A major-league swing," Scott's father declared. "All those years of batting practice with me finally paid off."

"Just don't teach her your pickoff move," Scott said. "Okay, Dad? Keep that in the family."

His father shook his head. "It's a great move," he declared.

"It sure is," Miri said. "That's the move I used to throw the tin out the window!"

"Miri, do you feel up to talking to the police now?" her mother asked. "We really should go down there and give them your statement. I promised them we would right after supper."

Miri nodded. "I feel fine, honest," she said.

So the three of them drove down to the police station and walked in together. What none of them was expecting was the standing ovation that greeted them as they entered.

"Hey, Miri, care to join the force?" one of the police officers asked.

Miri blushed, but she felt proud too. Sure she knew the robber was going to be there. But she could have bungled the whole business, and Pop could be in the hospital, or worse. She'd done well, and she was just starting to know it. The knowledge felt good.

One of the police officers took her statement, and Miri was relieved when no hard-to-answer questions were asked. Her story made sense, she realized. Thank goodness her mother had sent her to get Pop home early. And it was a good thing, too, that the robber had looked so much like a robber. Otherwise Miri would have had to explain why she knew to hide at the sight of him. But the ski mask and the gun were explanation enough.

"You know kids who perform heroically can get medals," the police officer who was writing down Miri's statement told her. "I forget whether Congress hands them out or the President, but there's a big ceremony when it happens. You know, a kid rescues another one who's drowning or gets a family out of a burning house. I'd be happy to find out about it and write you up for the medal if you want."

"Oh no," Miri said. It felt dishonest to her. Most people when they performed their rescues didn't have any forewarning. "I didn't really know what I was do-ing," she continued. "I just got so angry at the way that robber kept calling Pop an old man that I had to hit him one. I wasn't being heroic. Just mad."

"You behaved very levelheadedly for someone who was acting out of anger," the police officer declared. "Throwing that tin out the window was brilliant."

"He was going to shoot," Miri said. "I heard that click, and I knew I had to do something. I'm just glad I did the right thing."

"You're one brave girl," the police officer said. "Now are you brave enough to face all the reporters who want to talk to you?"

"Do I have to?" Miri asked.

"I would," the police officer replied. "They're going to pester you until you do, so you might as well get it over with, and then your life can get back in order."

"All right," Miri said. If she could tell the story to the police without bringing the VCR into it, she sup-posed she could manage the same with the reporters.

She was surprised there were so many of them though. At least a half dozen were milling around waiting for her to show up. There was even a TV crew there.

"We'll have to ask the Forrests to tape tonight's

news," Miri's mother whispered. "That way we can watch Miri on the VCR over and over again."

Miri grinned. It seemed like such a wonderful way to use a VCR, just to tape something with it.

The reporters made a big fuss about how courageous and quick-witted she was. Miri answered their questions as best she could. She relaxed as soon as she realized none of them were going to bother her about time travel because it wouldn't occur to any of them to even think to ask about it. But she still held on to her mother and Pop while the reporters asked away. Their flesh felt warm and solid as they held hands.

"Any advice for other victims of crime, Miri?" one of the reporters asked.

"Are you kidding?" Miri replied. "I'm only eleven. I'm not going to give advice like that to grown-ups."

That seemed to satisfy the reporters, and they all laughed and applauded and put away their notebooks and recording devices. Miri answered another couple of quick questions about where she went to school, and what the score of the softball game had been, and then she, her mother, and Pop finally were able to leave.

They drove home not talking very much. At one point Pop turned on the radio, and there on the news they heard the story of Miri and how she had rescued her grandfather.

"Don't let this go to your head," Pop said. "By tomorrow everybody will have forgotten all about it."

"Everybody except us," her mother said. "I think we'll remember for at least two more weeks."

Miri grinned. For the next twenty-four hours at least, if she wanted to remember what it felt like to be a celebrity, all she had to do was press the rewind button on the VCR. She wouldn't change a thing either when she went back. Not eat a single cracker.

They went straight back to their house, and Miri's mother made some warm milk to calm them down. The phone rang just as they sat down at the kitchen table. Miri answered it and was relieved to hear Kelly's voice.

"You okay?" Kelly asked her.

"I'm just fine," Miri replied.

"We've got to get together real soon to talk about baseball," Kelly declared. "There are a lot of things we have to decide about it."

"I know," Miri said. "But not tonight, Kelly. All right?"

"I know not tonight," Kelly said. "Scott, stop hitting me. He's punching me in the arm. Scott, stop it!"

Miri giggled.

"Tomorrow night then," Kelly said. "Even Scott agrees we have to talk. And not at school either. We have to figure out just what we're going to do."

"Tomorrow night," Miri said. "I'll talk to you at school about it."

"Great," Kelly said. "Miri, Scott and I are really proud of you."

"Thanks, Kel," Miri said, hanging the phone up fast so she wouldn't cry.

"What about tomorrow night?" Miri's mother asked.

"Oh nothing," Miri said. "You know Kelly. She just wants me to come over when things are less crazy and talk about everything that happened tonight."

"There's certainly plenty to talk about," Pop said. "I haven't seen so much excitement since D day."

"No more excitement tonight, please," Miri's mother said. "Now why don't we all drink this nice warm milk, and then when it takes us forever to fall asleep at least we won't have to drink any more of it."

"Fair enough," Miri said, and she drank her milk. When they all had finished they said good night to each other and prepared for bed.

Miri climbed into bed and tossed and turned. She tried to think about everything that had happened as though she were Kelly and making notes about it. She only wished she knew what had become of the missing time. But that sense of emptiness was a small price to pay for having Pop alive and well.

There was a soft knock on her door and Miri immediately called, "Come in."

Pop opened the door. "I couldn't sleep," he said. "It was a long day."

Miri nodded.

"Something funny happened today at the store," Pop declared. "When the gun went off."

"What, Pop?" Miri asked.

"I felt the bullet hit me," Pop said. "In my chest."

"But it didn't," Miri said, trying not to panic. "You're all right, aren't you?"

"I'm fine," Pop said. "The bullet didn't come anywhere near me. But I felt it, just for a second. A burning explosion inside."

"I wonder why," Miri said. "You don't think it was your heart, do you?"

Pop shook his head. "I think it might have had something to do with mutant machines," he said softly. "The kind that make you watch the *Margie Maclain Show* over and over."

"That could be, Pop," Miri said.

"Tomorrow," Pop said. "There'll be time enough to talk about it tomorrow."

"Okay," Miri said. "Good night, Pop."

"Good night, Miri," Pop said. "And thank you for all the tomorrows you've given me."

Miri watched as Pop closed the door behind him. Now there were four who knew, four to figure out what to do with their knowledge. She could feel the tension leave her body, and with a small smile she turned her face to the wall, closed her eyes, and let sleep take her to where she belonged.

About the Author

Susan Beth Pfeffer is the author of many books for young readers, including *Courage, Dana; Just Between Us;* and *What Do You Do When Your Mouth Won't Open? Rewind to Yesterday* is the first of two books about time travel.

Ms. Pfeffer was born in New York City and now lives in Middletown, New York.